NEVER TOO FAR

Abbi Glines

SIMON & SCHUSTER

London · New York · Sydney · Toronto · New Delhi

A CBS COMPANY

This edition published in the UK in 2013 by Simon & Schuster UK Ltd
A CBS COMPANY

Simon & Schuster UK Ltd
1st Floor
222 Gray's Inn Road
London WC1X 8HB

Simon & Schuster Australia, Sydney
Simon & Schuster India, New Delhi

A CIP catalogue record for this book is available from the British Library.

ISBN: 978-1-47113-468-5
E-BOOK ISBN: 978-1-47111-862-3

www.simonandschuster.co.uk

Printed and bound by CPI Group (UK) Ltd, Croydon CR0 4YY

For information concerning the cover art please visit Sarah Hansen's website at http://okaycreations.net/site/
Initial editor: Stephanie T. Lott a.k.a. Bibliophile

Abbi loves to hear from her readers. You can connect with her on
Facebook: Abbi Glines (Official Author Page)
Twitter: @abbiglines
Website: www.abbiglines.com

PROLOGUE

13 YEARS AGO . . .

There was a knock at the door, then just the small shuffle of feet. My chest already ached. Mom had called me on their way home to tell me what she'd done and that now she needed to go out to have some cocktails with friends. I'd be the one that would need to soothe Nan. My mom couldn't handle the stress it involved. Or so she'd said when she called me.

"Rush?" Nan's voice called out with a hiccup. She'd been crying.

"I'm here, Nan." I said as I stood up from the beanbag I'd been sitting on in the corner. It was my hiding spot. In this house you needed a hiding spot. If you didn't have one then bad things happened.

Strands of Nan's red curls stuck to her wet face. Her bottom lip quivered as she stared up at me with those sad eyes of hers. I hardly ever saw them happy. My mother only gave her attention when she needed to dress her up and show her off. The rest of the time she was ignored. Except by me. I did my best to make her feel wanted.

"I didn't see him. He wasn't there," she whispered then a small sob escaped. I didn't have to ask who "he" was. I knew. Mom had gotten tired of hearing Nan ask about her father. So she'd decided to take her to see him. I wish she'd told me. I wish I could have gone. The stricken look on Nan's face had my hands balling into fist. If I ever saw that man I was gonna punch him in the nose. I wanted to see him bleed.

"Come here," I said reaching out a hand and pulling my little sister into my arms. She wrapped them around my waist and squeezed me tightly. Times like this it was hard to breathe. I hated the life she'd been given. At least I knew my dad wanted me. He spent time with me.

"He has other daughters. Two of them. And they're . . . beautiful. Their hair is like an angel's hair. And they have a momma that let's them play outside in the dirt. They were wearing tennis shoes. Dirty ones." Nan was envious of dirty tennis shoes. Our mother didn't allow her to be less than perfect at all times. She'd never even owned a pair of tennis shoes.

"They can't be more beautiful than you," I assured her because I firmly believed that.

Nan sniffed and then pulled back from me. Her head tilted up and those big green eyes looked up at me. "They are. I saw them. I could see pictures on the wall with both girls and a man. He loves them . . . He doesn't love me."

I couldn't lie to her. She was right. He didn't love her.

"He's a stupid asshat. You have me, Nan. You'll always have me."

BLAIRE

PRESENT DAY . . .

Fifteen miles out of town was far enough. No one ever came this far out of Sumit to visit a pharmacy. Unless of course they were nineteen and in need of something they didn't want the town to know they had purchased. Everything bought at the local pharmacy would be spread throughout the small town of Sumit, Alabama within the hour. Especially, if you were unmarried and purchasing condoms . . . or a pregnancy test.

I put the pregnancy tests up on the counter and didn't make eye contact with the clerk. I couldn't. The fear and guilt in my eyes was something I didn't want to share with a random stranger. This was something I hadn't even told Cain about.

Since I forced Rush out of my life three weeks ago I'd slowly fallen back into the routine of spending all my time with Cain. It was easy. He didn't press me to talk and when I did want to talk, he listened.

“Sixteen dollars and fifteen cents,” the lady on the other side of the counter said. I could hear the concern in her voice. Not surprising. This was the purchase of shame all teenage girls feared. I handed her a twenty dollar bill without lifting my eyes from the small bag she’d placed in front of me. The one that held the one answer I needed yet was terrified of. Ignoring the fact my period was two weeks late and pretending like this wasn’t happening was easier. But I had to know.

“Three dollars and eighty-five cents is your change,” she said as I reached out and took the money in her outstretched hand.

“Thanks,” I mumbled and took the bag in front of me.

“I hope it all turns out okay,” the lady said in a gentle tone. I lifted my eyes and met a pair of sympathetic brown eyes. She was a stranger that I’d never see again but in that moment it helped having someone else know. I didn’t feel so alone.

“Me too,” I replied before turning from her and walking toward the door and back out into the hot summer sun.

I’d taken two steps into the parking lot when my eyes fell on the driver’s side of my truck. Cain stood there leaning against it with his arms crossed over his chest. The grey baseball cap he was wearing had a University of Alabama A on it and was pulled down low shading his eyes from me.

I stopped and stared at him. There was no lying about this. He knew I hadn’t come here to buy condoms. There was only one other option. Even without the ability to see the expression in his eyes I knew that he knew.

Swallowing the lump in my throat that I'd been fighting since I got in my truck this morning and headed out of town, I forced myself to put one leg in front of the other. Now it wasn't just me and the stranger behind the counter that knew. My best friend knew too. He'd ask questions and I would have to answer. After the past few weeks Cain deserved an explanation. He deserved the truth. But how did I explain this?

I stopped just a few feet in front of him. I was glad the hat shaded his face. It would be easier to talk if I couldn't see his thoughts flashing in his eyes.

I wanted him to speak first, but after what felt like several minutes of silence I knew he was waiting for me to say something.

"How did you know where I was?" I finally asked.

"You're staying at my grandmother's. The moment you left acting strange she called me. I was worried about you," he replied.

Tears stung my eyes. I would not cry about this. I'd cried all I was going to cry. Clenching the bag holding the pregnancy test closer to me I straightened my shoulders. "You followed me," I said. It wasn't a question.

"Of course I did," he replied then shook his head and turned his gaze away from me to focus on something else. "Were you gonna tell me, Blaire?"

Was I going to tell him? I didn't know. I hadn't thought that far. "I'm not sure there is anything to tell just yet," I replied honestly.

Cain shook his head and let out a hard low chuckle that held no humor. "Not sure, huh? You came all the way out here because you weren't sure?"

He was angry. Or was he hurt? He had no reason to be either. "Until I take this test I'm not sure. I'm late. That's all. There was no reason I should tell you about this. It isn't your concern."

Slowly Cain turned his head back to level his gaze on me. He lifted his hand and tilted his hat back. The shade was gone from his eyes. There was disbelief and pain there. I hadn't wanted to see that. It was almost worse than seeing the judgment I'd expected.

"Really? That's how you feel? After all we've been through that's how you honestly feel?"

What we had been through was in the past. He was my past. I'd been through a lot without him. While Cain had enjoyed his high school years I'd struggled to hold my life together. What exactly did he think he'd suffered through? Anger slowly boiled in my blood and I lifted my eyes to glare at him.

"Yes, Cain. That's how I feel. I'm not sure what *exactly* you think we've been through. We were best friends, then we were a couple, then my momma got sick and you needed your dick sucked so you cheated on me. I had to take care of my sick momma alone. No one to lean on. Then she died and I left. I got my heart and world shattered and came home. You've been here for me. I didn't ask you to, but you have and I'm thankful for that, but it doesn't make all that other stuff go away. It doesn't make up for the fact you deserted me when I needed you the most. So excuse me if when my world is once again about to be jerked out from under me that you aren't the first person I run to. You've not earned that yet."

I was breathing hard and the tears I hadn't wanted to shed were running down my face. I hadn't wanted to cry dammit. I closed the distance between us and used all my strength to shove Cain out of my way so I could grab the door handle and jerk it open. I needed out of here. Away from him.

"Move," I yelled, as I tried hard to open the door with his weight still against it.

I expected him to argue with me, but he moved without saying a word. I climbed inside the driver's seat and threw the little plastic bag in the seat beside me before cranking the truck and backing out of the parking spot. I could see Cain still standing there. He wasn't looking at me. He was staring at the ground as if it had all the answers. I couldn't worry about him right now. I needed to get away.

Maybe I shouldn't have said those things to him. Maybe I should have kept them inside where I'd buried them all these years. But it was too late now. He'd pushed me at the wrong moment. I would *not* feel bad about this.

I also couldn't go back to his grandmother's. She was on to me. Cain would probably call her and tell her. If not the truth something close to it. I didn't have any other options. I was going to have to take a pregnancy test in the restroom at a service station. Could this get any worse?

RUSH

The waves crashing against the shore used to soothe me. I'd been sitting out here on this deck watching the water since I was kid. It had always helped me find a better perspective on things. That wasn't working for me anymore.

The house was empty. My mother and her husband, the man who I wanted to burn in Hell for all fucking eternity, had left as soon as I got back from Alabama three weeks ago. I'd been angry, broken and wild. After threatening his life, I demanded they leave. I didn't want to see either of them. I needed to call my mom and talk to her but I couldn't bring myself to do that just yet.

Forgiving my mom was easier said than done. Nan, my sister, had stopped by several times and begged me to talk to her. This wasn't her fault but I couldn't talk to her about it either. She reminded me of what I'd lost. What I'd barely had. What I never expected to find.

A loud banging came from inside the house and broke into my thoughts. Turning I looked back and realized that someone was at the door as the doorbell chimed followed by knocking again. Who the hell was that? No one had stopped by except my sister and Grant since Blaire had left.

I sat my beer down on the table beside me and stood up. Whoever it was they needed a real good reason for coming over here uninvited. I walked through the house that had stayed clean since Henrietta's, the house cleaner, last visit. With no parties or social life it was easy to keep things from getting destroyed. I was finding I liked this much better.

The knocking started up again on the door just as I reached it. I jerked it open ready to tell whoever it was to fuck off when words failed me. This wasn't someone I expected to ever see again. I'd only met the guy once and I instantly hated him. Now he was here, I wanted to grab him by the shoulders and shake him until he told me how she was. If she was okay. Where she was living? God I hoped she wasn't living with him. What if he'd . . . no, no, no, that hadn't happened. She wouldn't. Not *my* Blaire.

My hands clenched tightly into fists at my sides.

"I need to know one thing," Cain, the boy from Blaire's past, said as I stared at him in confused disbelief. "Did you," he stopped and swallowed. "Do you . . . *fuck*—" He took off his baseball cap and ran a hand through his hair. I noticed the dark circles under his eyes and the tired weary expression on his face.

My heart stopped and I reached out and grabbed his upper arm and shook him, "Where's Blaire? Is she okay?"

"She's fine . . . I mean she's okay. Let go of me before you break my damn arm," Cain snapped, jerking his arm away from me. "Blaire is alive and well in Sumit. That isn't why I'm here."

Then why was he here? We had one connection. Blaire.

"When she left Sumit, Blaire was innocent. Very innocent. I had been her only boyfriend. I know how innocent she was. We've been best friends since we were kids. The Blaire that came back wasn't the same as the one that left. She doesn't talk about it. She *won't* talk about it. I just need to know if you and her . . . if y'all . . . I'm just gonna say this, did you fuck her?"

My vision blurred as I moved without any thought other than to murder him. He'd crossed a line. He wasn't allowed to talk about Blaire like that. He wasn't allowed to ask those kinds of questions or doubt her innocence. Blaire was innocent damn him. He had no right.

"Holy shit! Rush, bro, put him down!" Grant's voice called out to me and I heard him but it was far away and in a tunnel. I was focused on the guy in front of me as my fist connected with his face and blood spewed from his nose. He was bleeding. I needed him to bleed. I needed someone to fucking bleed.

Two arms wrapped around mine from behind and pulled me back as Cain stumbled backwards holding his hands up to his nose with a panicked look in his eyes. Well, one of his eyes the other one was already swelling shut.

"What the hell did you say to him?" Grant asked Cain from behind me, his arms holding me in a vice-like grip.

"Don't you fucking say it!" I roared when Cain opened his

mouth to reply. I couldn't hear him talk about her like that. What we had done was more than something dirty and wrong. He acted like I'd ruined her. Blaire was innocent. So incredibly innocent.

Grant's arms tightened on me as he pulled me back against his chest. "You need to go now." He said to Cain. "I can only hold him for so long. He's got about twenty more pounds of muscle on him than I do and this ain't as easy as it looks. You need to run, dude. Don't come back. You're one lucky shit I showed up."

Cain nodded and turned and headed back to his truck stumbling some as he went. The anger had simmered in my veins but I still felt it. I wanted to hurt him more. To wash any thought he may have in his head that Blaire wasn't as perfect as she had been when she had left Alabama. He didn't know what she'd been through. The hell my family had inflicted on her. How could he take care of her? She needed me.

"If I let you go are you gonna chase his truck down or are we good?" Grant asked loosening his hold.

"I'm good," I assured him as I shrugged free of his arms and walked over to the railing to grip it and take several deep breaths. The pain was back full force. I'd managed to bury it until it only throbbed a little but seeing that chickenshit reminded me of everything. That night. The one I would never recover from. The one that would mark me forever.

"Can I ask you what the hell that was about or are you gonna beat the shit outta me too?" Grant asked putting some distance between us.

He was my brother for all intents and purposes. Our parents had been married when we were kids. Long enough for us to form that bond. Even though my mom had a couple husbands since then Grant was still my family. He knew enough to know this was about Blaire.

"Blaire's ex-boyfriend," I replied without looking back at him.

Grant cleared his throat. "So, uh, he come over here to gloat? Or did you just beat him to a bloody pulp because he touched her once?"

Both. Neither. I shook my head. "No. He came over here asking questions about me and Blaire. Things that weren't his business. He asked the wrong thing."

"Ah, I see. That makes sense. Well he paid for it. The dude's probably got a broken nose to go with that black eye of his."

I finally lifted my head and looked back at Grant. "Thanks for pulling me off him. I just snapped."

Grant nodded then opened the door. "Come on. Let's go turn on the game and have a beer."

BLAIRE

My mother's grave was the only place I could think of to go. I had no home. I couldn't go back to Granny Q's. She was Cain's grandmother. He was probably there waiting on me. Or maybe he wasn't. Maybe I'd pushed him away too. I sat down at the foot of my mother's grave and pulled my knees up under my chin, wrapping my arms around my legs.

I had come back to Sumit because it was the only place I could think of to run to. Now, I needed to leave. I couldn't stay here. Once again my life was about to take a sudden change. One I wasn't prepared for.

When I'd been a little girl my momma had taken us to Sunday school at the local Baptist church. I remembered a scripture they read us from the Bible about God not putting more on us than we could bear. I was beginning to wonder if that was just for those people who went to church every

Sunday and prayed before they went to bed at night. Because He wasn't holding back any punches with me.

But feeling sorry for myself wasn't going to help me. I had to figure this out. My staying with Granny Q and letting Cain help me deal with day to day life had only been temporary. I knew when I moved into her guest bedroom I couldn't stay long. There was too much history between Cain and me. History I didn't intend to ever repeat. The time to leave was here, but I was still just as clueless about where I was gonna go and what I was gonna do as I had been three weeks ago. And seeing those pink lines on the pregnancy tests hadn't made a decision any easier.

"I wish you were here, Momma. I don't know what to do and I don't have anyone to ask," I whispered as I sat there in the quiet cemetery. I wanted to believe she could hear me. I didn't like the idea of her being under the ground but after my twin sister, Valerie, had died I'd sat here in this spot with my mom and we'd talked to Valerie. Momma had said her spirit was watching out for us and she could hear us. I so wanted to believe that now.

"It's just me left. I miss y'all. I don't want to be alone . . . but I am. And I'm scared." The only sound was the wind rustling the trees. "You once told me if I listened real hard I'd know the answer in my heart. I'm listening Momma, but I am so confused. Maybe you could help me out by pointing me in the right direction somehow?"

I rested my chin on my knees and closed my eyes refusing to cry.

"Remember when you said I needed to tell Cain exactly how I felt. That I wouldn't feel better until I had it all out. Well, I did just that today. Even if he does forgive me for that it'll never be completely. I can't keep relying on him for things anyway. It's time I figure this out on my own. I just don't know how."

Just asking her made me feel better. Knowing I wouldn't get an answer didn't seem to matter.

A car door slammed breaking the peacefulness and I dropped my arms from my legs and turned to look back at the parking lot to see a car that was way too expensive for this little town. Turning my eyes to see who had stepped out of it I gasped then jumped up. It was Bethy. She was here. In Sumit. In the cemetery . . . driving a very, very expensive looking car.

Her long brown hair was pulled over her shoulder in a ponytail. There was a smile tugging on her lips as my eyes met hers. I couldn't move. I was afraid I was imagining things. What was Bethy doing here?

"You not having a cell phone is a pain. How the hell am I supposed to call you and tell you I'm coming to get your ass if I have no number to call? Hmmm?" her words made no sense but just hearing her voice sent me running the short distance between us.

Bethy laughed and opened her arms as I flung myself into them. "I can't believe you're here," I said after squeezing her.

"Yeah, well, me either. That was one long drive. But you're worth it and seeing as you left your cell phone in Rosemary I had no way to talk to you."

I wanted to tell her everything but I couldn't. Not yet. I needed time. She knew about my dad already. She knew about Nan. But the rest . . . I knew she didn't know.

"I'm so glad you're here but how did you find me?"

Bethy grinned and tilted her head to the side. "I drove through town looking for your truck. It wasn't that hard. This place has like one red light. If I had blinked twice I'd have missed it."

"That car probably caught some attention coming through town," I said glancing over at it.

"It's Jace's. That thing rides like a dream."

She was still with Jace. Good. But my chest ached. Jace reminded me of Rosemary. And Rosemary reminded me of Rush.

"I'd ask you how you are, but, girl, you look like a walking stick figure. Have you eaten since you left Rosemary?"

My clothes were all falling off me. Eating had been difficult with the large knot that stayed tight in my chest at all times. "It's been a rough few weeks but I think I'm getting better. Moving on from things. Dealing with it."

Bethy shifted her gaze to the grave behind me. Both of them. I could see the sadness in her eyes as she read both the headstones. "No one can take away your memories. You have those." She said reaching over and taking my hand in hers and squeezing.

"I know. I don't believe what they told me. My father is a liar. My mother wouldn't have done what they claim. If anyone is to blame it is my father. He caused this pain. Not my momma. Never my momma."

Bethy nodded and held my hand firmly in hers. Just having someone listen to me and know they believed me. That they believed my mother's innocence helped.

"Did your sister look a lot like you?"

The last memory I had of Valerie was of her smiling. That bright smile that was so much prettier than mine. Her teeth were perfect without the help of braces. Her eyes were brighter than mine. But everyone said we were identical. They didn't see the difference. I always wondered why. I could see it so clearly.

"We were identical," I replied. Bethy wouldn't understand the truth.

"I can't imagine two Blaire Wynn's. Y'all must have broken hearts all over this little town." She was trying to lighten the mood after asking about the sister I'd lost. I appreciated it.

"Just Valerie. I was with Cain from the time I was young. I didn't break any hearts."

Bethy's eyes went a little wide, then she glanced away before clearing her throat. I waited until she turned back to me. "Although seeing you is awesome and we could totally rock this town, I'm actually here for a purpose."

I'd assumed she was, I just couldn't figure out what that purpose was exactly.

"Okay," I said waiting for more of an explanation.

"Can we talk about it over a coffee," she frowned then

glanced back at the street. "Or maybe the Dairy K since that's like the only place I saw when I drove through town."

She wasn't comfortable hanging out amongst the graves like I was. That was normal. I was not. "Yeah, okay," I said and walked over to pick up my purse.

"There's your answer," a soft voice whispered so quietly I almost thought I'd imagined it. Turning to look back at Bethy she was smiling with her hands tucked in her front pockets.

"Did you say something?" I asked, confused.

"Uh, you mean after I suggested we go to the Dairy K?" she asked.

I nodded, "Yeah. Did you whisper something?"

She scrunched her nose and then glanced around nervously and shook her head. "Nope . . . um . . . why don't we get out of here?" she said reaching for my arm and pulling me behind her back toward Jace's car.

I looked back at my mom's grave and a peace settled over me. Had that been? No. Surely not. Shaking my head I turned back around and went to get into the passenger side before Bethy threw me in.

RUSH

It was my mother's birthday. Nan had called me twice already asking me to call Mom. I couldn't do it. She was on a beach in the Bahamas with *him*. This hadn't affected her at all. Once again she'd run off to enjoy her life while leaving her kids behind to figure things out.

"Nan's calling again. You want me to answer it and tell her to leave you the hell alone?" Grant walked into the living room holding up my cell phone in his hand while it rang.

Those two fought like actual brother and sister. "No, give it to me," I replied as he tossed me the phone.

"Nan," I said in greeting.

"Are you going to call mother or not? She has called me twice now asking me if I talked to you and if you remembered it was her birthday. She does care about you. Stop letting that girl ruin everything, Rush. She pulled a gun on me for God's sake. A gun, Rush. She is *crazy*. She—"

"Stop. Don't say anything else. You don't know her. You don't want to know her. So just stop. I'm not calling Mom. The next time she calls tell her that. I don't want to hear her voice. I don't *give a shit* about her trip or what she got for her birthday."

"Ouch," Grant muttered as he sank down on the couch across from me and propped his legs up on the ottoman in front of him.

"I can't believe you'd say that. I don't understand you. She can't be that good in—"

"Don't Nannette. This conversation is over. Call me if *you* need me."

I pressed end then slung my phone on the seat beside me and laid my head back on the cushion.

"Let's go out. Drink a little. Dance with some girls. Forget this shit. All of it," Grant said. He'd suggested this several times over the past three weeks. Or at least since I'd stopped breaking things and he felt it was safe enough to speak.

"No," I replied without looking at him. There was no reason to act like I was okay. Until I knew Blaire was okay, I was never going to be okay. She may not forgive me. Hell she may never look at me again but I needed to know she was healing. I needed to know something. Anything.

"I've been real good about not prying. I've let you go crazy, roar at everything that moved and sulk. I think it's time you told me something. What happened when you went to Alabama? Something had to of happened. You didn't come back the same."

I loved Grant like a brother but there was no way I was telling him about the night in the hotel room with Blaire. She'd been hurting and I'd been desperate. "I don't want to talk about that. But I do need to get out. Staring at these walls and remembering her . . . yeah I need to get out." I stood up and Grant jumped up from his spot on the couch. The relief in his eyes was obvious.

"What are you up for? Beer or girls or both?"

"Loud music," I replied. I really didn't need any beer and the girls . . . I just wasn't ready for that.

"We'll have to leave town. Maybe head to Destin?"

I threw my car keys at him, "Sure lead the way."

The doorbell rang stopping both of us. The last time I'd had an unexpected guest it hadn't ended well. It could very likely be the cops coming to arrest me for bashing Cain's face in. Oddly enough I didn't care. I was numb.

"I'll get it," Grant said glancing at me with a concerned frown. He was thinking the same thing.

I sat back down on the sofa and propped my feet up on the coffee table in front of me. My mom hated it when I put my feet on this table. She'd bought it during one of her international shopping trips and had it shipped back here. I felt a sudden pang of guilt for not calling her but I pushed it away. My entire life I'd made that woman happy and taken care of Nan. I wasn't doing that anymore. I was done. With all her shit.

"Jace, what's up? We were just headed out. You want to come with?" Grant said stepping back and letting Jace walk into the house. I didn't get up. I wanted him to leave. Seeing Jace reminded me of Bethy who then reminded me of Blaire. Jace needed to leave.

"Uh, no, I uh . . . I needed to talk to you about something," Jace said shuffling his feet and stuffing his hands in his pockets. He looked ready to bolt out of the door.

"Okay," I replied.

"Today might not be the best time to talk to him, man." Grant said stepping in front of Jace and focusing on me. "We were gonna head out. Let's go. Jace can bare his soul later."

Now I was curious. "I'm not a loose cannon, Grant. Sit down. Let him talk."

Grant let out a sigh and shook his head. "Fine. You wanna tell him this shit now then tell him."

Jace glanced over at Grant nervously before looking back at me. He walked over and sat down on the chair furthest from me. I watched as he tucked his hair behind his ear and wondered what he had to say that was such a big deal.

"Bethy and I are getting kinda serious," he started. I already knew this. I didn't care. I felt the pain crack open my chest and I clenched my fist forcing air into my lungs. Bethy had been Blaire's friend. She'd know how Blaire was. "And uh . . . well Bethy's apartment rent went up and that place was shitty anyway. I didn't feel safe with her staying there. So, I talked to Woods and he said that his dad had a two bedroom condo available if I wanted to rent that. I got it for her and paid the deposit and everything. But when I took her to see it she got pissed. Big time pissed. She didn't want me to pay her rent. She said it made her feel cheap." He sighed and the apologetic look in his eyes still made no sense. I didn't care about his fight with Bethy.

"It's twice as much as her last place – or Bethy thinks it is twice as much as her last place, it's actually four times as much. I'm paying the other portion without her knowing. I swore Woods to secrecy. Anyway. Bethy uh . . . she . . . took off to Alabama today. She loves the condo. She wants to live on the club property and on the beach. But she can't afford it without a roommate and the only person she would even consider having is . . . Blaire."

I stood up. I couldn't sit.

"Whoa man . . . sit down," Grant jumped up and I waved him off.

"I'm not mad. I just need to breathe," I said staring out the glass doors at the waves crashing against the shore. Bethy had gone to get Blaire. My heart was racing. Would she come back?

"I know the two of you had a real bad end. I asked Bethy not to go, but she got real mad and I don't like to upset her. She said she missed Blaire and that Blaire needed someone. She, uh, also talked to Woods about giving Blaire a job if she comes back."

Comes back . . .

She wouldn't come back. She hated me. She hated Nan. She hated my mom. She hated her father. She wouldn't come back here . . . but God I wanted her to. I turned my head and looked at Jace.

"Blaire won't come back," I said. The pain in my voice was undeniable. I didn't care about hiding it. Not anymore.

Jace shrugged.

"She may have had enough time to deal with things. What if she does come back? What will you do?" Grant asked me.

What would I do?

I'd beg.

BLAIRE

Bethy pulled Jace's car into the parking lot of the Dairy K. I noticed Callie's little blue Volkswagen and decided against getting out of the car. I'd only seen Callie twice since I returned to Sumit and she'd been ready to claw my eyes out. She'd had her sights on Cain since high school. I'd come home and messed up whatever kind of relationship they'd managed to finally have. I hadn't meant to. She could have Cain.

Bethy started to get out of the car and I reached over and grabbed her arm. "Let's just talk in the car," I said stopping her.

"But I want some ice cream mixed with Oreos," she complained.

"I can't talk out there. I know too many people," I explained.

Bethy sighed and leaned back in her seat. "Okay fine. My ass doesn't need any ice cream and cookies anyway."

I smiled and relaxed thankful for the dark tinted windows.

Knowing I wasn't on display as people stopped and stared at Jace's car. No one around here drove cars even close to this one's league.

"I'm not gonna beat around the bush with this, Blaire. I miss you. I've never had a close girlfriend before. Ever. Then you came along and then you left. I hate you being gone. Work sucks without you there. I have no one to talk to about my sex life with Jace and how sweet he's being, which is something I wouldn't even have if I hadn't listened to you. I just miss you."

I felt tears sting my eyes. Just being missed felt good. "I miss you too," I replied hoping I didn't get all weepy.

Bethy nodded and a smile tugged on her lips. "Okay good. Because I need you to come back and live with me. Jace got me a condo on the water on the club's property. I however refuse to let him pay for it. But I need a roommate. Please come back. I need you. And Woods said you'd have your job back immediately."

Go back to Rosemary? Where Rush was . . . and Nan . . . and my dad. I couldn't do that. I couldn't see them. They'd be at the club. Would my dad take Nan to play golf? Could I see that? No. I couldn't. It would be too much.

"I can't," I choked out. Wishing I could. I didn't know where I was going to go now that I was pregnant, but I couldn't go Rosemary and I couldn't stay here.

"Please, Blaire. He misses you too. He never leaves his house. Jace said he's pitiful."

The angry wound in my chest flared to life. Knowing Rush was hurting too was hard. I'd imagined him having his house parties and moving on. I didn't want him to still be sad. I just needed for us to move on. But now maybe I never would. I'd always have a reminder of Rush.

"I can't see them. Any of them. It would be too hard," I stopped. I couldn't tell Bethy about my pregnancy. I had hardly had time to comprehend it. I wasn't ready to tell anyone. I may never tell anyone other than Cain. I would be leaving here soon enough. Where I went I wouldn't know anyone. I'd be starting over.

"Your . . . uh Dad and Georgianna aren't there. They left. Nan is but she is quieter now. I think she's worried about Rush. It would be hard at first but after you ripped the band-age off of it you'd get over them. Over everything. Besides, the way Woods eyes lit up when I mentioned you coming back, you could distract yourself with him. He is *more* than interested."

I didn't want Woods. And nothing would distract me. Bethy didn't know everything. I couldn't tell her that either. Not today.

"As much as I want to . . . I just can't. I'm sorry."

I was sorry. Moving in with Bethy and getting my job back at the club would be the answer to my problems. Almost.

Bethy let out a frustrated sigh and laid her head back on the seat and closed her eyes. "Okay. I get it. I don't like it, but I get it."

I reached over and squeezed her hand tightly. I wished things were different. If Rush were just some guy I had broken up with it would be. But he wasn't. He never would be. He was more.

Bethy squeezed my hand back. "I'm going to let this go today. But I'm not looking for another roommate right away. I'm giving you a week to think about this. Then I have to find someone to help me pay the bills. So will you? Think about it?"

I nodded because I knew that was what she needed even if I knew her waiting was pointless.

"Good. I'll just go home and pray you'll change your mind – that is if God even remembers who the hell I am." She winked at me and then reached across the seat to hug me. "Eat some food for me, okay? You're getting too skinny."

"Okay," I replied wondering if that were going to be possible.

Bethy sat back. "Well if you aren't gonna pack up and head back to Rosemary with me then at least let's go out. I can't do that drive again today. We can go find some fun somewhere and then crash at a hotel tonight."

I nodded. "Yes. That sounds good. Just no honky tonks." I couldn't walk into another one of those. At least not this soon.

Bethy frowned. "Okay . . . but is there anything else in this state?"

She had a point. "Yeah . . . we can drive into Birmingham. It's the closest big city."

"Perfect. Let's go have some fun."

* * *

When we pulled into the driveway at Granny Q's she was sitting outside on the porch shelling peas. I didn't want to face her, but she had given me a roof over my head for three weeks with no strings attached. She deserved an explanation if she wanted one. I wasn't sure Cain had told her anything. His truck wasn't here and I was immensely grateful.

"Want me to stay in the car?" Bethy asked. It would be easier if she did but Granny Q would see her and call me out for being rude for not letting my friend come inside.

"You can come with me," I told her and opened the car door.

Bethy walked around the front of the car and fell into step beside me. Granny Q hadn't looked up from her peas yet but I knew she'd heard us.

I looked over at her as she continued to shell those peas in silence. Her white hair that she kept cut off in a short bob was all I could see of her. No eye contact. She was thinking about what she was going to say. Cain must have told her. Dang it. It would be so much easier to just go inside and take advantage of her not speaking to me. But this was her home. If she didn't want me here I needed to pack up and leave.

"Hey, Granny Q," I said and stopped waiting for her to lift her head to look at me.

Silence. She was upset with me. Disappointed or mad I wasn't sure. I hated Cain right now for telling her. Couldn't he keep his mouth shut?

"This is my friend Bethy. She came to visit me today," I continued.

Granny Q finally raised her head and gave Bethy a smile then turned her eyes on me. "You take her on in and fix her a nice big glass of ice tea and give her one of them fried pies I got cooling on the table. Then you come on back out here and talk to me a minute, hmmm." This wasn't a request it was a subtle demand. I nodded and led Bethy inside.

"Did you piss off the old lady?" Bethy whispered when we were safely inside.

I shrugged. I wasn't sure. "Not real sure just yet," I replied.

I went to the cabinet and got a tall glass down and went to fixing Bethy a glass of ice tea. I didn't even ask her if she wanted it. I was just trying to do what Granny Q had said.

"Here. Drink this and eat a fried pie. I'll be back in a few minutes," I said and hurried past her back outside. I needed to get this over with.

BLAIRE

The wooden planks cracked under my feet as I stepped back onto the front porch of Granny Q's house. I let the screen door close behind me with a loud bang before remembering it was old and its springs were long ago rusted. I'd spent many days of my childhood on this front porch shelling peas with Cain and Granny Q. I didn't want her upset with me. My stomach twisted.

"Sit down girl and stop looking like you're ready to cry. God knows I love ya like you're my own. Thought you would be one day," she shook her head. "Stupid boy couldn't get it together. I hoped he'd wake up 'fore it was too late. But he didn't did he? You done gone and found someone else."

This had not been what I was expecting. I took the seat across from her and reached into the metal bucket between us and began shelling peas so I wouldn't have to look at her. "Cain and

I were over three years ago. Nothing that is happening now is affecting that. He is my friend, that's all."

Granny Q made a hmph sound and shifted in the porch swing she was sitting in. "I don't believe that. You two were inseparable as kids. Even as a boy he couldn't keep his eyes off you. It was funny to watch how much he adored you and didn't even realize it himself. But boys hit them teenage years and lose their ever loving minds. I hate that he did. That he lost you, girl, 'cause there won't be another Blaire for Cain. You were it for him."

She hadn't mentioned my pregnancy tests. Did she even know I'd bought them? I didn't want to recap my past with Cain. Sure we had history but there was so much sadness and regret in that past, I didn't want to go there. I'd been living in a lie my father had constructed then. Remembering it hurt. "Has Cain come by here today?" I asked.

"Yeah. He came by this morning looking for ya. I told him you'd not come back home from your early escape. He looked worried and turned and left without telling me anythin' else. He'd been crying though. Don't reckon I've ever seen him cry before. Least not since he was a boy."

He'd been crying? I closed my eyes and dropped the peas into the large plastic bucket by Granny Q. Cain wasn't supposed to be upset. He wasn't supposed to cry. He'd let me go a long time ago. Why was this so hard on him? "How long ago was that?" I asked thinking about the hours that had passed since I'd bared my soul to him in the parking lot of the pharmacy.

"Ah, 'bout nine hours ago I'd guess. It was early. He was a mess, girl. At least go find him and talk to him. No matter how you feel about him now he needs to hear that things are okay from you."

I nodded. "Can I use your phone?" I asked standing up.

"Of course you can. Eat you one of them fried pies while you're in there. I made enough for an army after Cain ran off this morning. They're his favorite flavor," she said.

"Cherry," I replied and she gave me a smile. I could see so many things in those eyes of hers. I knew Cain. I understood him. We had a past. I loved his family and they obviously loved me too. That, at least, was safe.

Bethy was standing on the other side of the door sipping her glass of sweet tea and holding her phone out to me. She'd been listening. I wasn't surprised.

"Call the boy. Get this over with," she said.

I took her phone and walked into the living room to give myself some privacy before dialing Cain's number. I knew it by heart. He'd had the same number since he got his first cell phone when we were sixteen.

"Hello," came his reply. I could hear the hesitation in his voice. Something was off. He sounded like he was talking through his nose.

"Cain? Are you okay?" I asked suddenly worried about him.

There was a pause then a long sigh, "Blaire. Yeah . . . I'm fine."

"Where are you?"

He cleared his throat. "I, uh . . . I'm in Rosemary Beach."

He was in Rosemary? What? I sank down on the sofa behind me and gripped the phone tighter. Was he telling Rush? My heart slammed against my chest and I closed my eyes tightly before asking, "Why are in you in Rosemary? Please tell me you didn't . . ." I couldn't say it. Not with Bethy in the other room more than likely listening.

"I needed to see his face. I needed to see if he loved you. I . . . I just needed to know." That made no sense.

"What did you say? How did you find him? Did you find him?" Maybe he hadn't found him. Maybe I could stop this.

There was a hard chuckle on the other end of the line. "Yeah, I found him alright. Ain't real hard. This place is small and everyone knows where the rock star's son lives."

Oh god, oh god, oh god . . . "What did you say to him?" I asked slowly as horror washed over me.

"I didn't tell him. I wouldn't do that to you. Give me some damn credit. I cheated on you because I was a horny-ass teenage boy but dammit, Blaire, when are you gonna forgive me? Will I pay for that mistake the rest of my life? I'm sorry! GOD I'm so *fucking* sorry. I would go back and change everything if I could." He stopped and made a grunt that sounded like he was hurting.

"Cain. What's wrong with you? Are you okay?" I asked. I didn't want to acknowledge what he'd said. I knew he was sorry. I was too. But, I was never going to get over it. Forgiving was one thing. Forgetting was another.

"I'm fine. I'm just a little battered. Let's just say the guy isn't crazy about me, okay."

Had Rush hurt him? That didn't sound like Rush at all. "I don't understand."

"It's okay. I got a room for the night and I'm sleeping this off. I'll be home tomorrow. We have some things to talk about."

"Cain. Why did Rush hurt you?"

Another pause and then a weary sigh. "Because I asked questions that he didn't think were my business. I'll be home tomorrow."

He'd asked questions? What kind of questions?

"Blaire, you don't have to tell him. I'll take care of you. Just . . . we need to talk."

He'd take care of me? What was he talking about? I wasn't going to let him take care of me. "Where are you exactly?" I asked.

"Some hotel just outside of Rosemary. They think their shit don't stink in that town. Everything there cost five prices too much."

"Okay. Stay in bed and I'll see you tomorrow." I replied then hung up.

Bethy stepped into the room. She cocked one of her dark eyebrows as she stared at me waiting. She'd been listening. I'd known she would.

"I need a ride to Rosemary," I told her standing up. I couldn't let Cain lay hurt in a hotel room and I couldn't chance that he'd go back and try to talk to Rush again. If Bethy could drive me there, I could check on him then drive him home.

Bethy nodded and a small smile tugged on her lips. I could tell she didn't want me to see how happy she was to hear this. But I wasn't planning on staying. She didn't need to get her hopes up. "This is just about Cain. I'm not . . . I can't stay there."

She didn't appear to believe me. "Sure. I know."

I wasn't in the mood to convince her. I handed her the phone and headed back to my temporary bedroom to pack some things.

RUSH

Grant had finally given up on me and gone to dance with one of the girls who had been flirting with us since we walked into the club. He'd come here for some fun and I'd needed the distraction, but now that I was here I just wanted to leave. Taking a drink of my beer I tried not to make eye contact with anyone. I kept my head down and a scowl on my face. It wasn't hard to do.

Jace's words kept replaying in my head. I was scared . . . no I was terrified to let myself believe that Blaire would come back here. I'd seen her face that night in the hotel room. She was empty. The emotion in her eyes was gone. She had been finished – with me, with her father, with everything. Love was cruel. So *fucking* cruel.

The bar stool beside me scrapped across the floor as it was moved back. I didn't look over at it. I didn't want anyone to talk to me.

"Please tell me that ugly scowl on your pretty face isn't over a girl. You might break my heart," the smooth female voice was familiar.

I tilted my head to the side just enough to see her face. Although she was older now I recognized her immediately. Meg Carter. There are some things a guy doesn't forget in life and the girl who takes his virginity is one of them. She'd been three years older than me and visiting her grandmother the summer I turned fourteen. It hadn't been a love connection. More like a life lesson.

"Meg," I replied, relieved it wasn't another unknown female here to throw herself at me.

"And he remembers my name. I'm impressed," She replied then looked up at the bartender and smiled. "Jack and Coke please."

"Guy doesn't forget his first."

She shifted on her stool crossing her legs and tilting her head to look at me causing her long dark hair to fall over one shoulder. She still wore it long. I'd been fascinated with it back then.

"Most guys don't, but you've led a different life compared to most guys. The fame has to have changed you over the years."

"My dad's famous not me," I snapped hating it when girls wanted to talk about something they knew nothing about. Meg and I had fucked a few times but she didn't really know much about me.

"Hmmm, whatever. So, why you so glum?"

I wasn't "glum". I was a broken mess. But Meg wasn't

someone I intended to unload on. "I'm good," I replied and glanced back at the dance floor hoping to catch Grant's attention. I was ready to go.

"You look like you've got a broken heart from hell and don't know what to do with it," she said then reached for her Jack and Coke to take a sip.

"I'm not gonna talk to you about my personal life, Meg." I let the warning edge in my voice ring through loud and clear.

"Whoa there, handsome. I wasn't trying to piss you off. Just making small talk."

My personal life wasn't small talk. "Then ask me about the fucking weather," I said with a snarl.

Meg didn't respond and I was glad. Maybe she'd move on. Leave me alone.

"I'm in town taking care of my Grans. She's sick and I needed something new to do with my life. I just went through a bad short messy divorce. A change of scenery from Chicago was what I needed. I'll be here for at least six months. Do you think you'll be ornery the entire time I'm here or are you gonna get nicer anytime in the near future?"

She wanted to see me. No. I wasn't ready for that. I started to reply when my phone went off in my pocket alerting me to a text message. Relieved to have an interruption so I could think about how I was going to respond I pulled it out of my pocket. The number wasn't one I recognized. But the "Hey, It's Bethy" caught my attention and I stopped breathing as I opened the text to read the entire thing.

Hey, it's Bethy. If you aren't a stupid fuck then you'll wake up and get with the program.

What the hell did that mean? What was I missing? Was Blaire in Rosemary? Is that what this meant. I stood up and put enough money on the bar to cover my beer and Meg's drink. "I gotta go. It was nice to see you. Take care," I said as an after thought before I stalked through the crowd until I found Grant having dry humping some redhead on the dance floor.

His eyes met mine and I nodded at the door. "Now," I said and turned to head outside. I was leaving him here if he hadn't caught up with me by the time I reached my Range Rover. She could be here. I was going to find out. Asking Bethy what she meant by that jacked up text was pointless.

BLAIRE

I reached over and nudged Bethy's leg to wake her up. She'd been asleep for the past two hours. We were just outside of Rosemary Beach and I needed her to drive so I could look for Cain's truck at all the inexpensive motels.

"We there?" she mumbled sleepily and sat up in her seat.

"Almost. I need you to drive. I gotta look for Cain's truck."

Bethy let out a weary sigh. I knew she was only doing this in hopes of getting me to Rosemary and keeping me there. She couldn't care less about finding Cain, but I'd needed a ride. I was going to drive Cain home. And he and I were going to talk. He had no business coming out here to see Rush. I only hoped Cain hadn't told him about what he'd caught me buying.

It wasn't that I wanted to keep it a secret from Rush. It was just that I hadn't let everything sink in yet. I needed to process it. Figure out what I wanted to do. Then I'd contact Rush. Cain going after him like a crazy person was not what I wanted. I still couldn't believe he'd done it.

"Pull over here. I need to run in and grab me a latte first," Bethy instructed. I did as she asked and parked the car in front of Starbucks.

"You want something?" Bethy asked as she opened the door. I wasn't sure that caffeine was good for the . . . for the baby. I shook my head and waited until she got out of the car until I let out the sob in my chest I hadn't been expecting. I hadn't thought about those two pink stripes and what they really meant. *A baby*. Rush's baby. Oh God.

I stepped out of the car and walked around the front to get into the passenger side. By the time I was back in the car and buckled up Bethy was headed back to the car. She looked a little more awake already. I pushed thoughts of my baby back and focused on finding Cain. I could dwell on my future . . . on our future later.

"Okay. I have caffeine. I'm ready to find this dude."

I didn't say anything. I knew she knew his name by now. I'd used it several times. She was just refusing to acknowledge it. This was her form of rebellion. Cain represented Sumit and she didn't want me in Sumit. Instead of aggravating me it warmed me. She wanted me with her. I felt wanted and it was nice.

"He left Rosemary because of the price of hotel rooms. So, he's somewhere affordable. Can you take me to a few of those?" I asked.

She nodded, but didn't look at me. She was texting. Great. I needed her to focus and she was more than likely telling Jace we were almost there. I didn't really want Jace to know anything.

We drove around for thirty minutes with me checking parking lots at all of the cheap motels in town. Still no Cain. This was getting frustrating. He had to be here somewhere.

"Can I use your phone? I'm gonna call him again and let him know I'm here looking for him. He'll tell me where he is when he knows I've driven all this way."

Bethy handed me her phone and I quickly dialed Cain's number. It rang twice.

"Hello?"

"Cain. It's me. Where are you? I'm just outside of Rosemary and I can't find your truck anywhere."

There was silence, then "Dammit."

"Don't get all mad. I needed to check on you. I came out here to drive you home." I knew he'd be frustrated that I came this close to Rosemary again.

"I told you I'd be home once I slept it off, Blaire. Why couldn't you have stayed put?" the aggravation in his voice annoyed me. You would think he was happy I'd come to check on him.

"Where are you, Cain?" I asked again. Then I heard it. A female voice in the background. The phone became muffled. It didn't take a genius to figure out Cain was with a girl and he was trying to hide it from me. This pissed me off. Not because I was jealous, but because he'd let me think he was hurt and alone in a strange city. Asshole.

"Listen. I don't have time for more of your stupid ass games, Cain. I've been there done that. Next time could you not make it sound like you need me when it's obvious you don't."

"Blaire, no. Listen to me. It isn't what you think. I couldn't sleep after you called so I got back in the truck and headed home. I wanted to see you."

An angry scream came from the other side of the phone. He was pissing off whoever he was with. The boy was an idiot.

"Go make your company feel better. I don't need an explanation. I don't need anything from you. I never did."

"BLAIRE! NO! I love you, baby. I love you so much. Please listen to me," he begged and the girl with him got more hysterical. "Shut up, Callie!" he roared and I knew then he was back in Sumit. He was with Callie.

"You went to Callie? You came home so I wouldn't worry and went to see Callie? You're ridiculous, Cain. For real? This doesn't hurt me. You can't hurt me anymore. But think about others feelings for a change. You keep jerking Callie around and it's wrong. Stop thinking with your penis and grow up."

I pressed end and handed Bethy back her phone. Her eyes were wide as she stared at me. "He went back to Sumit," I said in way of explanation.

"Yeah . . . I got that part," Bethy said slowly. She was waiting for more. She deserved more. She'd brought me back here. She was also the only real friend I had. Cain wasn't a friend. Not really. A friend wouldn't keep doing stupid stuff like he did.

"Can I sleep at your place tonight? I don't think I'm going back to Sumit. I was leaving soon anyway. I'll figure out where I'm going tomorrow and then when I get there I'll have Granny Q ship the rest of my things. It isn't like I have that much anyway. My truck is headed to the graveyard. It would never make the trip again."

Bethy nodded and cranked up the car then pulled out onto the road. "You can stay with me as long as you need. Or longer," she replied.

"Thank you," I said before laying my head back on the seat and taking a deep breath. What was I going to do now?

The smell of bacon got thicker and thicker the more I inhaled. It was as if bacon was taking over my senses. My throat constricted. My stomach rolled from the rich smell of it. The grease sizzled somewhere in the distance. Before I could completely get my eyes open my feet were on the floor and I was running to the bathroom.

Luckily Bethy's apartment wasn't big and I didn't have far to run.

"Blaire?" Bethy's voice called from the kitchen but I couldn't stop.

Dropping to my knees in front of the toilet I gripped the porcelain seat with both hands and began throwing up everything in my stomach until nothing but dry heaves wracked my body. Every time I thought I was finished I'd smell the bacon grease mixed with my vomit and it would begin again.

I was so weak my body trembled as I tried to vomit and nothing else would come up. Suddenly a cold washcloth was on my face and Bethy was standing over me flushing the toilet and then leaning me back against the wall.

I held the cloth over my nose to block out the smell of bacon and Bethy noticed and closed the bathroom door behind her. After she turned on the fan she put her hands on her hips and stared down at me. The disbelief on her face confused me. I got sick. What was so strange about that?

"Bacon? The smell of bacon made you hurl?" she shook her head still staring at me as if she couldn't believe it. "And you weren't gonna tell me were you? You were just gonna put your crazy ass on some damn bus and leave. All by yourself. I can't believe you, Blaire. What happened to the smart girl that taught me not to let a man use me? Hmmm? Where the hell did she go? 'Cause your plan here sucks. Like bad. You can't just run off. You have friends here and you're gonna need friends. I'd hope that you intend to tell Rush about this too. I know you well enough to know that this is his baby."

How did she know? I just threw up. Lots of people get viruses. "It's a virus," I muttered.

"Don't lie to me. It was the *bacon*, Blaire. You were sleeping so peacefully on the couch and the minute I started cooking you started making weird noises and tossing and turning. Then you shot off like a bullet to puke your guts out. Not rocket science, baby. Get that shocked look off your face."

I couldn't lie to her. She was my friend. Possibly my only one now. I pulled my knees up to my chin and wrapped my arms around my legs. This was my way of holding myself together. When I felt like the world was breaking around me and I couldn't control it I always held together this way.

"That's why Cain came here. He caught me buying pregnancy tests yesterday. I know that's why he came, to ask Rush . . . to ask about the relationship between Rush and I. It's something I refused to talk to Cain about. I didn't want to talk about Rush at all. Then I was late. Two weeks late. I thought I'd buy a couple of tests and they would be negative and everything would be okay." I stopped my explanation and rested my cheek against my knees.

"The tests . . . they were positive?" Bethy asked.

I nodded but didn't look up at her.

"Were you gonna tell Rush? Or were you really gonna just run off?"

What would Rush do? His sister hated me. His mother hated me. They hated my mother. And I hated my father. For Rush to be a part of this baby's life he'd have to give them up. I couldn't ask him to give up his mom and sister. Even if they were evil. He loved them. And he wouldn't give up Nan. I'd already learned that when it came to me or Nan, he'd choose Nan. He had up until the end. When I'd found out everything. He'd kept her secret. He'd chosen her.

"I can't tell him," I said quietly.

"Why is that exactly? Because he'd want to know and his ass needs to be a man and be there for you. This running off shit is stupid."

Bethy didn't know everything. She only knew bits and pieces. It had been Nan's story to tell and no one else's in Rush's eyes. But I disagreed. It was my story too. Nan still had both her parents and her brother. I had no one. My mother was dead. My sister was dead. And my father might as well be dead. So this story was just as much mine as it was hers. Maybe more so.

I lifted my head and looked up at Bethy. She was my one friend in the world and if I was going to tell this story then it was her I wanted to tell it to.

RUSH

It had been three weeks, four days and twelve hours since I'd seen her. Since she'd torn my heart out. If I had been drinking, I'd blame it on the alcohol. It had to be an illusion; a desperate one. But I hadn't been drinking. Not a drop. There was no mistaking Blaire. It was her. She was actually here. Blaire was back in Rosemary. She was at my house.

I'd spent five hours last night driving all over the damn place searching for Bethy hoping she'd lead me to Blaire. But I hadn't found either of them. Coming home and admitting defeat had been painful. I had convinced myself Bethy was still in Sumit with Blaire. That maybe the text from Bethy had been a drunken text and nothing more.

I soaked in the sight of her. She was thinner and I didn't like it. Was she not eating? Had she been sick?

"Hello, Rush," she said breaking the silence. The sound of her voice almost sent me to my knees. God I'd missed that voice.

"Blaire," I managed to say terrified that I'd scare her away just by speaking.

She reached up and wrapped a strand of her hair around her finger and tugged on it. She was nervous. I didn't like that I was making her nervous. But what could I do to make this easier? "Can we talk?" she asked softly.

"Yeah," I stepped back to let her in. "Come inside."

She paused and glanced past me toward the house. The fear and pain flashing in her eyes had me silently cursing myself. She'd been hurt here. Her world had been destroyed in my house. *Dammit*. I didn't want her to feel this way about my house. Not when there were good memories here too.

"Are you alone?" she asked. Her eyes shifted back to me.

She didn't want to see my mom or her dad. I got it now. It wasn't the house. "I forced them to leave the day you left," I replied, watching her carefully.

Her eyes went wide. Why did this surprise her? Didn't she get it? She came first. I'd told her as much in that hotel room. "Oh. I didn't know . . ." she trailed off. We both knew she didn't know because she'd cut me from her life.

"It's just me. Except for Grant's occasional visits it's always just me." She needed to know I hadn't moved on. I wasn't interested in moving on.

Blaire walked into the house and I clenched my hands into fists as her familiar sweet scent followed her. So many nights I'd sat here and dreamed of seeing her walk back into my life. My world.

"Can I get you something to drink?" I asked thinking how I really wanted to beg her to talk to me. To stay with me. To forgive me.

Blaire shook her head and turned around to look at me. "No. I'm good. I . . . I just . . . I was in town and well," she scrunched her nose and I fought the urge to reach up and touch her face. "Did you hit Cain?"

Cain. *Shit* she knew about Cain. Was she here to talk about Cain? "He asked things he shouldn't have. Said things he shouldn't have," I replied through my clenched teeth.

Blaire sighed. "I can only imagine," she mumbled and shook her head. "I'm sorry he came here. He doesn't think things through. He just acts on impulse." She wasn't defending him. She was apologizing for him. That wasn't her job. The stupid fucker wasn't her responsibility or her fault.

"Don't apologize for him, Blaire. It makes me want to hunt his ass down," I growled unable to control my reaction.

"It's my fault he was here, Rush. That's why I'm apologizing. I upset him and he assumed it was all because of you so he came running here before talking things out with me."

Talking things out with her? What the fuck did Cain need to talk out with her? "He needs to back off. If he so much as —"

"Rush. Calm down. We are old friends. Nothing more. I told Cain some things I've needed to say for a long time. He didn't like it. I was cruel but I needed to say them. I was tired of protecting his feelings. He pushed me too far. That's all it was."

I took a deep breath but the pounding in my head had gotten louder.

"Did you come to see him?" I needed to know if that was why she was here. If this had nothing to do with me then my heart needed to deal with it.

Blaire walked over toward the steps instead of going into the living room. I noticed it. I understood. She might have come in my house but she couldn't walk in there and face things. Not yet. Maybe never. "He may have been my excuse to get into the car with Bethy," she paused and let out a sigh. "But he was gone when I got here. I stayed for other reasons. I . . . I need to talk to you."

She'd come here to talk to me. Had it been enough time? I used every ounce of will power I possessed to stand still and not go pull her into my arms. I didn't care what she had to say. The fact she wanted to see me was enough. "I'm glad you came," I said simply.

The small frown was back and Blaire wouldn't look directly at me. "Things are still the same. I haven't been able to let it go. I'll never be able to trust you. Even . . . even if I want to. I can't."

What the fuck did that mean? The pounding in my ears grew stronger.

"I'm leaving Sumit. I can't stay there. I've got to make it on my own," she added.

What? "Are you moving in with Bethy?" I asked wondering if I was still asleep and this was a dream.

"I wasn't going to, but this morning I talked with her and I thought maybe if I saw you and talked to you and faced . . . this, I'd be able to stay with her for a while. It won't be permanent. I would be leaving in a couple months. Just until I had time to decide where I was going to go next."

She was still planning on leaving. I needed to change that. I had a couple months if she stayed here. For the first time since she'd told me to leave the hotel room I had hope. "I think that's smart," I said. "No reason to make a rash decision when you have an option right here." She could stay in my house for free. In my bed. With me. But I couldn't offer that. She'd never agree.

BLAIRE

"I'll be working at the club. We'll . . . uh . . . see each other on occasion. I'd get a job somewhere else, but I need the kind of money the club pays." I was explaining this to myself as much as I was explaining it to Rush. I hadn't been sure exactly what I was going to say when I showed up here. I just knew I had to face him. At first Bethy had begged me to tell him about the pregnancy. After she'd heard exactly what happened that day with my father, Nan and Rush's mother she hadn't been as Team Rush as before. She agreed that there was no need to tell him anything right away.

Working up enough nerve to actually drive back to this house after the way I'd left only three and a half weeks ago had been hard. The hope that my heart wouldn't react when I saw Rush's face had been futile. My chest had constricted so badly it had been a wonder I could breathe. Much less speak. I was pregnant with his baby . . . our baby. But the lies. The deceit. Who he was. All of that kept me from saying the words that he deserved to hear. I couldn't. It was wrong. I was being selfish. I knew it. But it didn't change anything. I couldn't let the way I felt about him cloud my decisions for my future . . . my baby's future. My father. Rush's mother and sister. They would never be a part of my baby's life. I wouldn't allow it. I couldn't.

"Of course. Yeah, working at the club is good money," he stopped and ran a hand through his hair. "Blaire, nothing's changed. Not for me. Having you here again. Seeing your face. God, baby, I can't do this. I can't pretend I'm not fucking thrilled you're standing in my house right now."

I couldn't look at him. Not now. I hadn't been expecting him to say any of those things. The stilted nervous conversation was more of what I expected. It was what I wanted. My heart couldn't take anything else. "I need to go, Rush. I can't . . . I just wanted to make sure you were good with me being in town. I'll keep my distance."

Rush moved so fast I didn't realize it until he was standing between me and door. "I'm sorry. I was trying to be cool. I was trying to be careful, but I cracked. I'll do better. I promise. Go to Bethy's. Forget what I just said. I'll be good. I promise. Just . . . just don't leave. Please."

What did I say to that? He managed to make me want to comfort him. To apologize to him. He was lethal to my emotions and good sense. Distance. We needed distance. I nodded and stepped around him. "I'll . . . uh . . . probably see you around." I managed to croak out before opening the door and stepping outside the house.

I didn't look back but I knew he was watching me leave. It was the only reason I didn't break out into a run. Space . . . we needed space. And I needed to cry.

It was as if he had known I was coming. I'd already decided to go straight to the dining room and look for Jimmy. I figured Jimmy would know where to find Woods. But Woods had been waiting on me at the door when I opened the back entrance to the country club's restaurant and clubhouse.

"And she returns. Honestly I didn't think you would," Woods drawled as the door closed behind me.

"For a little while maybe," I replied.

Woods winked at me then nodded his head toward the hall that led down to his office. "Let's go talk."

"Okay," I said as I followed him.

"Bethy's already called me twice today. Wanting to see if I'd seen you yet. Making sure you got your job back," Woods said as he opened his office door and held it so that I could walk inside. "What I didn't expect though was the call I just received about ten minutes ago. It surprised me. From the way you bolted out of here three weeks ago and left Rush all high and dry, I didn't expect him to call me on your behalf. Not that he needed to mind you. I'd already agreed that you could have your job back."

I stopped and looked back at him. Had I just heard him correctly? "Rush?" I asked almost afraid I'd hallucinated that comment.

Woods closed his door and walked over to stand in front of his desk. He leaned back against the expensive looking shiny wood and crossed his arms over his chest. The smile he'd had when I arrived was gone. He looked more concerned now. "Yes, Rush. I know that the truth came out. Jace has told me some of it. What he knows at least. But then I already knew who you were. Or who Rush and Nan thought you were. I warned you he'd choose her. He was already choosing her when I gave you that warning. Do you really want to come back to all of this? Is Alabama that bad?

No. Alabama wasn't that bad. Being a single, pregnant, ninetee-year-old with no family was bad though. That however was not something I was going to share with Woods. "Coming back here isn't exactly easy. Seeing . . . them, won't be easy either. But I need to figure out what I'm going to do. Where I'm going to go. There is nothing left for me in Alabama. I can't stay there and pretend that there is. It's time I found a new life. And Bethy is the only friend I have. My options on places to go are a little limited."

Woods eyebrows shot up. "Ouch. What am I? Here I thought we were friends."

Smiling I walked over and stood behind the chair across from him. "We are, but, well . . . not close friends."

"Not because I didn't try my damndest."

A small laugh bubbled up and Woods grinned. "That's nice to hear. I missed it."

Maybe coming back wouldn't be so hard.

"You can have your job. It's yours. I've had shit for cart girls and Jimmy is still sulking. He doesn't play well with the other servers. He misses you too."

"Thank you," I replied. "I appreciate it. I want to be honest with you though. In four months, I intend to leave. I can't stay here forever. I've . . ."

"You have a life to get to. Yeah, I heard you. Rosemary isn't where you intend to put down your roots. I got it. For whatever length of time, you got the job."

RUSH

I knocked once before opening the door to Nan's condo and walking in. Her car was parked outside. I knew she was here. I just wanted to make sure if she had company that she also knew I was about to walk in on them. I'd made the mistake once of not knocking and seeing my little sister straddling a guy's lap. I had wanted to pour bleach in my eyes and brain after that experience.

"Nan, it's me. We need to talk." I called out then closed the door behind me. I stepped into the living room and the sound of more than one hushed voice and footsteps coming from the master bedroom almost made me turn around and leave. But I wasn't going to. This was more important. Her sleepover guest needed to go on home now anyway. It was after eleven.

Her bedroom door opened and closed. Interesting. Whoever was here was staying. We'd need to step outside on the balcony to talk. I wasn't discussing Blaire in front of anyone else. I probably knew the guy in that room. It would be the only reason she would keep him hidden in there.

"Ever heard of calling before you come over?" Nan snapped as she walked into the living room dressed in a short silk wrap. She looked so much like our mother the older she got.

"It's almost lunch, Nan. You can't keep the man in bed all day," I replied and opened the doors that led out onto the balcony overlooking the gulf. "I need to talk to you and I don't want to do it so that your bedroom buddy can hear us."

Nan rolled her eyes and stepped outside. "I find it odd that I've been trying to get you to talk to me for weeks and now that *you* want to talk you come barging over like I have no life. At least I call you first." She was starting to sound like our mother too.

"I own this condo, Nan. I can come in any damn time I want to," I reminded her. She would be leaving here in mid-August to head back to her sorority house and her still undecided major. College was a social function for her. She knew I'd pay her bills and tuition. I'd always taken care of everything for her.

"Snarky much. What is this about? I haven't had my coffee yet." She also wasn't afraid of me. I didn't want her to be, but it was time she grew up. I wasn't going to let her send Blaire running. In a month, Nan would be gone. Normally I would too. Not this year. I'd be keeping my residence at Rosemary. Mother would have to pick another location. She wasn't going to have this house free for the rest of the year.

"Blaire is back," I told her bluntly. I'd had time to see things from another angle. I didn't feel like Nan was the victim in this any longer. As a child she was, but then so was Blaire. Nan tensed as her eyes flashed with the hate that belonged at her father's feet instead of on Blaire. "Don't say anything. Let me speak first or I'll go escort your sleepover friend from my condo. I hold the power here, Nan. Our mother has nothing. I support you both. I've never asked you for anything. Ever. But right now I'm going to ask . . . No I'm going to demand you listen to me and you follow my terms."

Nan's anger had faded and now the spoiled brat was there looking back at me. She didn't like being told what to do. I couldn't blame my mother for her behavior, not entirely. I did this too. Overcompensation had ruined Nan.

"I hate her," she seethed.

"I said to listen to me. Don't assume I'm bluffing, Nan. This time you've fucked with something I care about. This affects me, so listen and shut the hell up."

Her eyes went round from shock. I was sure I'd never spoken to her that way. I was even a little surprised myself. Hearing the hate in her voice directed at Blaire had set me off.

"Blaire is staying with Bethy. Woods has given Blaire her job back. She has nothing in Alabama. She has no one. The father the two of you share is worthless. And to her he might as well be dead. She's back to find out where she fits and what to do next. She was doing that before but when the truth came out it sent her world crumbling so she ran. It's a fucking miracle she's back here. I want her back here, Nan. You may not want to hear this but I love her. I will stop at *nothing* to make sure she's safe. She is secure and no one and I do mean no one, not even my sister, makes her feel unwanted. You leave soon for college. You can keep your misplaced hate if you want to but one day I hope you grow up enough to realize there is only one person to hate here."

Nan sank down onto one of the lounge chairs she kept out on the balcony to lay out and read books. I loved her too. I'd been protecting her all my life. Telling her this and threatening her was hard, but I couldn't let her hurt Blaire any longer. I had to stop this. Blaire would never give me another chance as long as Nan was tormenting her life.

"So you're choosing her over me," Nan whispered.

"This isn't a contest Nan. Stop acting like it is. Let it go."

Nan lifted her eyes and tears were clinging to her eyelashes. "She's made you hate me."

Damn fucking drama. Nan lived a soap opera at least in her head. "Nan listen to me. I love you. You're my little sister. No one can change that. But I am *in love* with Blaire. It may be a major hitch in your plans to conquer and destroy but, baby, it is time you let your daddy issues go. Three years ago he came back. I need you to put this behind you."

"What about family first?" She chocked out.

"Don't go there. You and I both know I've put you first all my life. You needed me and I was there. But we are adults now Nan."

She wiped her tears and stood back up. I could never tell if her tears were real or fake. She could turn them on and off at whim. "Fine. Maybe I'll go back to school early. You don't want me here anyway. You've chosen her."

"I'll always want you around, Nan. But this time I want you to play nice. Think about someone else for a change. You have a heart. I've seen it. Now it is time to use it."

Nan's spine stiffened. "If we're done here could you please leave *your* condo?"

I nodded. "Yeah I'm done," I replied and walked back inside. Without another word I headed out the front door. Time would now tell if I had to actually follow through on my threats to teach my sister a lesson. I really hoped I didn't.

BLAIRE

I needed my things and I needed to sell my truck. It would never make it this far again. Cain had checked it out for me last week after it broke down and said he could temporarily fix it. The cost to fix all that was wrong with it would be more than I could afford to spend. Calling and asking Granny Q or Cain to ship my things and sell my truck seemed wrong. They deserved an explanation in person . . . or at least Granny Q did. She'd given me a roof, a bed and fed me for three weeks. I was going to have to go back to Sumit to get my stuff and say goodbye to Granny Q. Woods had given me a few days to get settled in before I started back to work.

Bethy had taken off yesterday to take me to apply for Medicaid. It was time I saw a doctor but I would need insurance first. Today I had overheard her tell Jace she was looking forward to their date tonight. I'd been monopolizing all her time since she came and got me. I was beginning to feel like a lot of work. I hated that feeling. I could take a bus. It would be affordable and I wouldn't be a burden on Bethy.

A knock on the door interrupted my thoughts. I went to open it and was surprised to find Rush standing there with his hands tucked into the front of his jeans and one of his tight Tshirts on. He reached up and pulled off his aviator sunglasses. I wished he'd kept them on. The silver color of his eyes in the sunshine was even more breathtaking than I remembered.

"Hey, I saw Bethy at the clubhouse. She said you were here," Rush explained. He was nervous. I'd never seen Rush nervous.

"Yeah . . . um Woods gave me a couple of days to get my things from Sumit before I start back to work."

"You've got to go and get your things?"

I nodded, "Yeah. I just brought an overnight bag with me when I left. I hadn't exactly been planning on staying."

Rush frowned. "So how are you going to get there? I don't see your truck."

"I was just about to Google bus stations and see where the closest one to here is."

Rush's frown deepened. "It's forty minutes away. All the way in Fort Walton Beach."

That wasn't as bad as I'd feared.

"A bus isn't safe Blaire. I don't like the idea of you taking a bus. Let me take you. Please. I'll get you there faster and I would be free. You could save your money."

Ride with him? All the way to Sumit and back? Was that a good idea?

"I don't know . . ." I trailed off because honestly I didn't know. My heart wasn't ready for that much Rush.

"We don't even have to talk . . . or we can if you want. I'll let you choose the music and I won't complain."

If I went back with Rush, then Cain wouldn't put up a fight. Or then again he could. He could tell Rush about the pregnancy. But would he? I never even told him the results of the tests.

"I know you can't forgive the lies and the hurt. I'm not asking you to. You know I'm sorry and if I could go back and change things I would. Please, Blaire, just as a friend who wants to help and keep you safe from crazy men who could hurt you on a bus, let me drive you."

I thought of how very unlikely it was that I'd get hurt on the bus. And then I thought about the fact I wasn't just keeping myself safe anymore. I had another life to protect inside of me.

"Okay. Yes. I'd like a ride."

Jace was sprawled out in the large stuffed blue chair that sat in Bethy's living room with his feet propped up on the ottoman and Bethy curled up in his lap. I was on the sofa feeling like a science experiment as they both stared at me in confusion.

"So you're fine with Rush taking you to Sumit to get your things tomorrow? I mean you don't feel weird or . . ." Bethy trailed off.

It would be strange. It would also hurt just being near him but I needed a ride. Bethy needed to work, not take another day off to help me this week. "He offered. I needed a ride so I said yes."

"And it was that easy? Why am I not buying it?" Bethy asked.

"Because she's leaving out the parts where he begged and pleaded," Jace said with a chuckle.

I pulled the afghan up over my shoulders. I was cold. I was cold a lot lately which was odd because it was summertime in Florida. "He didn't beg," I replied feeling an urge to defend Rush. Even if he did actually beg.

"Yeah, right. If you say so," Jace took a drink of the sweet tea Bethy had fixed him.

"It isn't our business. Leave her alone, Jace. We need to decide on what to do about the lease on this place ending in a week."

I wouldn't be here long. I'd told her that. Moving into the more expensive condo wasn't a good idea. My half of the rent wouldn't be covered after I left and she'd be left with all of it.

Jace picked up Bethy's hand and kissed it then grinned at her. "I told you I'd take care of things. If you'd just let me," he winked at her and I turned my head away. I didn't want to watch them. Rush and I had never been like that. Our relationship had been short. Intense and brief. I wondered what it would have felt like to have the freedom to curl up in Rush's arms anytime I wanted. To know I was safe and that he loved me. We never had that chance.

"And I told you I'm not going to let you pay my rent. Sorry. New plan. Oh, Blaire why don't we go apartment hunting tomorrow?"

A knock on the door interrupted me before I could reply. Then Grant opened the door and walked in.

"You did not just walk into my girl's apartment without permission. She could've been naked." Jace snarled at Grant.

Grant rolled his eyes then flashed a smile in my direction. "I saw your car here, jackass. Calm down. I'm here to see if I can convince Blaire to take a walk with me."

"You trying to get your ass kicked?" Jace asked

Grant smirked and then shook his head before looking back at me. "Come on, Blaire, let's go take a walk and play catch up."

Had Grant been in on the lie? Surely he had known about it. I couldn't tell him no. Even if he had known he had also been the first nice person I met here. He'd filled my tank up with gas. He'd worried about me sleeping under the stairs. I nodded and stood up. "These two need some alone time anyway," I replied glancing back at Bethy. She was studying me closely. I gave her a reassuring smile and she appeared to relax.

"Don't leave on our account. We need to decide on where we're gonna live in a week," Bethy said as I walked to the door.

"Y'all can talk about that later, Bethy. Blaire's been gone for almost a month. You have to share," Grant replied opening the door for me to walk outside.

"Rush is gonna go apeshit," Jace called out right before Grant closed the door muffling whatever it was Bethy had started to say.

We walked down the stairs in silence. Once we were on the sidewalk I looked over at Grant. "Did you just miss me or is there something you want to say to me?" I asked.

Grant grinned. "I missed you. I've had to put up with Rush's sulking ass so trust me I missed the fuckin' hell outta you."

I could tell by his teasing tone he had wanted to make a joke. But thinking about Rush being upset didn't make me smile. It just reminded me of everything. "Sorry," I mumbled. I wasn't sure what else to say to that.

"Just glad you're back."

I waited. I knew there was more he wanted to say. I could sense it. He was taking his time and I figured he was trying to decide exactly how to say whatever it was he wanted to say to me.

"I'm sorry about what happened. How it happened. And Nan. She can come off as the world's biggest spoiled bitch but she's had a screwed up childhood. It warped her or something. If you'd lived with Georgianna as your mother you'd understand. Rush was a boy so he didn't get it as bad. But Nan, damn her world was fucked. It isn't an excuse for her just an explanation."

I didn't respond. I had nothing to say to that. I didn't feel sympathy of any kind for Nan. Obviously the men in her life did. Must be nice.

"Regardless of all that, what she did was wrong. How it was kept from you was really screwed up. I'm sorry I didn't say anything but honestly, I wasn't even aware you and Rush had anything going until that night at the club when he lost it over the snails. I'd noticed he was attracted to you, but so were most males in this town. I figured he was the one guy who wouldn't make a move on you because of his feelings for Nan . . . and well what you represented to the both of them." Grant stopped walking and I turned to look back at him.

"I've never seen him like this. Ever. It's like he's hollow. I can't get through to him. He doesn't smile. He doesn't even pretend to enjoy life anymore. He's different since you left. Even though he wasn't honest and it looks like he was just protecting Nan . . . you two just didn't have enough time. Nan has been his responsibility since he was a kid. That was all he knew. Then you came into his world and apparently rocked it overnight. If he'd had more time he would have told you. I know he would've. But he didn't. It wasn't fair to him. He was falling for this girl he had always thought had been the reason his sister was without a dad. His belief system was changing but it was hard for him to work through it too."

I just stared at him. Not because I didn't agree. I had already worked through all this in my head. I understood what Grant was saying. The problem was . . . it didn't change things. Even if Rush had been going to tell me, it didn't change who he was or who Nan was. What they represented to me. My mother's last three years on this earth had been hell while they lived in their fancy houses and lived from one social event to the next. Their belief in the lies they told me was the one thing I didn't think I could ever get over.

"Damn. I'm probably butchering this to shit. I just wanted to talk to you and make sure you knew that Rush . . . he needs you. He's sorry. And I don't think he's ever going to move on from you. If he tries to talk about it tomorrow at least hear him out."

"I've forgiven him, Grant. I just can't forget. What we were or what we were headed toward is over. It will never be again. I can't let it. My heart won't allow me to. But I'll always listen to him. I care about him."

Grant let out a weary sigh. "I guess that's better than nothing."

It was all I had to offer.

RUSH

Blaire came walking out of Bethy's apartment holding two cups of coffee before I could get out of the car. I opened my door and stepped out of the Range Rover. Her hair was loose and hanging down her back. I loved it like that. The shorts she had on barely covered up her legs which was going to make it hard to concentrate once she was sitting in my car. They would ride up her thighs. I tore my eyes off her legs and met her steady gaze. She was forcing a small smile.

"I brought you some coffee. Since you got out of bed so early for me. I know early isn't your thing." Her voice was unsure and soft as she spoke. It was going to be my mission to change that on this road trip. I wanted her comfortable with me again.

"Thank you," I replied with a smile I hoped would ease her nerves, as I opened the passenger side door for her. I'd been awake since three this morning unable to sleep. I was anxious. I was pretty sure I had gone through two pots of coffee since then. I wasn't about to tell Blaire that though. She'd brought me coffee. A real smile tugged on my lips as I closed her door and headed back to my side.

She was holding her cup up close to her mouth taking small sips when I glanced over at her. "If you want music, I promised it was all yours," I reminded her. She didn't move but a smile lifted the corners of her lips.

"Thanks. Trust me, I remember. I'm okay right now. You can listen to something if you want to. I need to wake up first."

I didn't care about the radio. I just wanted to talk. What we talked about wasn't important. Talking to her was all I cared about.

"So, what's the plan? Does Cain know we're coming to get your things?" I asked.

Blaire shifted in her seat and I forced myself to keep my eyes on the road and not her legs. "No. I wanted to explain to him and his grandmother, Granny Q, about this. She gave me a place to stay the past three weeks. I also need to convince him to sell my truck for me and send me the money. It won't make it back out here again. It's in bad shape."

Her truck was old. The idea that she wouldn't be riding around in it was a relief. However, I wasn't crazy about her not having a vehicle. How the hell I was supposed to fix that I didn't know. She would never take a car from me. Maybe her truck could be fixed and made safe.

"I could take it in and have it checked out while you're packing up. Could be it just needs a couple things done to it."

She sighed. "Thanks but don't bother. Cain already took it in and had it checked. He had them fix it up so I could get around town but he said it was a temporary fix. It was going to need more work than I could afford on it."

I gripped the steering wheel tighter. The idea that Cain had been taking care of her drove me insane. I hated that he'd been the one to have her truck checked out. That it was his family that helped her when she needed it most. Mine had fucked her life up. I wasn't there for her to call when she needed help.

"So are you and Cain . . . ?" What the hell was I asking? Where they what? Fuck. I didn't want to hear this.

"We are friends, Rush. We have been all our life. My feelings about him haven't changed."

I eased my grip on the steering wheel and ran one of my sweaty palms on my jeans. Damn she drove me crazy. If I was going to ease her back into being comfortable with me I needed to calm down. That was going to start with me not beating the shit outta Cain when I saw him.

Before I could say anything else Blaire leaned forward and turned on the radio. She found a country station on my satellite radio and then leaned back in her seat and closed her eyes. I had pried too much. She was politely asking me to shut up. I could take the hint.

Thirty minutes of silence had passed when my phone rang. Nan's name appeared on the screen in my dash. My damn iPhone was programmed to my car. Normally that came in handy and made things hands free, but having Blaire see Nan's name wasn't cool. I hadn't wanted a reminder of our issues. My plan was to make this day reminder free. I clicked ignore and the radio started playing again.

I didn't look over at Blaire but I felt her eyes on me. It was real hard not to meet her gaze.

"You could have talked to her. She's your sister," Blaire said so softly I almost missed it over the music.

"She is. But she represents things I don't want you thinking about today."

Blaire didn't stop looking at me. It was taking all my strength to keep this casual. Jerking the car over grabbing her face and telling her how important she was and how much I loved her wasn't what she needed right now.

"I'm better, Rush. I've had time to take everything in. Deal with it. I'll see Nan at the club. I'm prepared for that. You're helping me today. You could be doing anything else but you chose to take the day to help me. I don't want to keep you from taking phone calls from people you care about. I won't break."

Fuck. So much for keeping this casual and easy. I pulled over onto the side of the road and slammed the Rover into park. I kept my hands to myself but I gave my full attention to Blaire. "I chose to take you today because there is nothing I'd rather do than be near you. I'm driving you because I'm a desperate man who will take whatever the hell he can get when it comes to you." I broke down and reached over and ran my thumb over her cheekbone then into the silky hair I'd been fascinated with since I first laid eyes on her. "I will do anything. *Anything*, Blaire, just to be near you. I can't think about anything else. I can't focus on anything. So never think you're inconveniencing me. You need me, I'm there." I stopped. I sounded pathetic even to my own ears. Dropping my hand from her head I shifted the Rover back into gear and pulled back onto the road.

Blaire didn't say anything. I didn't blame her. I'd sounded like a crazy man. She was probably scared of me now. Hell, I would be.

BLAIRE

My heart was beating so hard I was sure Rush could hear it. This had been a bad idea. Being near him was so confusing. It was easy to forget who he was. Having him touch me even if it was just my face made me feel like crying. I wanted more than that. I missed him. Everything about him and I'd be lying if the idea of being this close to him all day hadn't kept me up most of the night.

Rush turned the radio back up when I didn't say anything. I should say something after his outburst but what? How did I respond to that without just causing us both more pain. Telling him I missed him and I wanted him wouldn't make this easier. It would just be harder.

This time when the phone rang the dashboard in his car flashed the name "Grant". Rush leaned up and pressed some button then picked up his cell phone.

"Hey," he said into the phone. I chanced a glance over at him since his focus was no longer on me. The hard frown lines in his face made me sad. I didn't want them there.

"Yeah. We're on our way," he replied into the phone. "Don't think that's a good idea. I'll call you when I'm back." His jaw clenched and I knew whatever Grant was saying was making him mad. "I said no," he growled then ended the call before tossing it into his cup holder.

"You okay?" I asked before I could think that through.

He jerked his head over to look at me. It was as if he was startled that I was talking to him. "Uh, yeah. I'm fine," he replied in a much calmer tone then turned his eyes back on the road.

I waited a few minutes then decided to say something about what he'd said to me. If I didn't start talking about this with him we would always have this awkward silence between us. Even if I left in four months and never saw him again . . . no I'd see him again. I would have to wouldn't I? Could I really never tell him about this baby? I pushed that back. I hadn't even been to the doctor yet. I'd cross that bridge when we got to it. Even if I had thrown up again this morning when I'd opened the trash compactor and gotten a whiff of the left over fried fish Jace had tossed last night. I wasn't normally so sensitive. The hot ginger tea I'd been drinking when Rush picked me up had helped ease my stomach. I could pretend like that pregnancy test was wrong or face the truth.

"About what you said. I, uh, I don't really know how to respond to that. I mean, I know how I feel and how I wish things were different, but they aren't. I want us to . . . I want us to find a way to be friends . . . maybe. I don't know. That sounds so lame. After everything," I stopped because my attempt at talking to him about this was sounding like a rambling mess. How could we be friends? That had been how all this started and here I was in love and pregnant by a man I could not build a future with.

"I'll be whatever you allow me to be, Blaire. Just don't shut me out again. Please."

I nodded. Okay. I'd give this friends thing time. Then . . . then I would tell him about the baby. He was either going to run like hell or want a part of our baby's life. Either way I needed time to prepare. Because I would not let my child have anything to do with his family, ever. It was out of the question.

I hated liars . . . but I was about to become one for a while. This time it was me that had a secret to keep.

"Okay," I replied but didn't say more. My eyes were growing heavy as the lack of sleep from last night and the fact I couldn't drink caffeine to wake me up started getting to me. I closed my eyes.

"Easy, sweet Blaire. Your head is falling over and you're gonna have one helluva cramp in your neck. I'm just laying your seat back," A deep warm whisper tickled my ear and I shivered. I turned toward it but I was still so sleepy I couldn't wake up completely. Something soft brushed my lips then I fell back into my dreams.

* * *

"You need to wake up, sleepyhead. I'm here but I have no idea where to go," Rush's voice accompanied by his hand gently squeezing my arm woke me. I rubbed my eyes and opened them. I was laying back. I looked over at Rush and he smiled.

"I couldn't let you jack up your neck. Besides, you were sleeping hard I wanted you to be comfortable. He unbuckled and reached across me to fiddle with a button on the side of my seat. It slowly eased back up and I could see the one traffic light in Sumit, Alabama in front of me.

"I'm so sorry. I slept the whole way. That had to be a boring ride."

"I got to control the radio so it wasn't a bust," Rush replied with a smirk and then looked back at the traffic light. "Where do I go from here?"

"Straight until you see the large wooden sign that is painted red and says "Fresh Produce and Firewood For Sale" then take a left. It's the third house on the right, but it takes about a mile and a half down that road to get there. The road will turn into gravel after about a quarter mile."

Rush followed my directions and we didn't say much. I was still waking up and my stomach was feeling queasy. I hadn't eaten yet and I knew that was the problem. I had saltine crackers in my purse that Bethy had given me but popping one of those in my mouth in front of Rush was a bad idea. Saltines were a major giveaway.

By the time we pulled into Granny Q's driveway I had

broken into a cold sweat. I was going to be sick if I didn't eat something. I opened the door to get out before Rush could see my face. I was probably green. At the very least pale.

"You want me to go with you or is it best if I stay here?" he asked.

"Oh, um . . . maybe you should stay here," I replied. Cain's truck was here so that meant he probably was too. I didn't want Rush and Cain getting into any more fights. I also didn't trust Cain to keep his mouth shut about the pregnancy tests. I closed the car door and headed for the house.

Cain opened the screen door and stepped outside before I even made it to the bottom step. His face was a mixture of worry and anger. "Why's he here? He brought you home now he can leave," Cain snarled looking past me toward Rush. Yeah it was a real good idea for Rush to stay in the car. My stomach rolled and I fought back the nausea.

"Because he's giving me a ride back. Calm down Cain. You have no fight with Rush. You're my friend. He's my friend. Let's you and I take this inside. I need to get my things."

Cain stepped back and let me pass him then he followed me inside letting the screen slam shut behind him.

"What do you mean you're going back with him? That test come back positive? You running back to him now even though he broke your heart so bad you came here three weeks ago a mess? I'll take care of you, Blaire. You know that."

I held up my hands to stop him. "This isn't about me being pregnant, Cain. He is a friend who gave me a ride. Yes we were more before . . . things happened but now we're not. I'm not running to him. I am getting my job back in Rosemary and living with Bethy for a while. Then I'll go somewhere else and start over. I just can't keep staying here."

"Why can't you stay here? Hell, Blaire I'll marry you today. No questions asked. I love you. More than life. You gotta know that. I messed up when we were younger and that thing with Callie she don't mean nothin' she's just a girl who distracts me. You're all I want. I've been telling you that for years. Please listen to me," he was begging now.

"Cain, stop this. You're my friend. What we had died a long time ago. I walked in on you doing things to another girl you shouldn't have been. That night everything changed. I love you but I am not in love with you and I never will be again. I need to pack and I need to move on with my life."

Cain slammed his hand against the wall. "Don't say that! It isn't over. You can't just run off on your own. It isn't safe," he paused, "Are you pregnant?" he asked.

I didn't answer. Instead, I walked back to the room I'd been staying in while I was here and grabbed my suitcase and started packing it.

"You are," he said following me into the room.

I didn't respond. I just focused on my things.

"Does he know? Is the rock star's son gonna take responsibility? He's lying, B. The baby will get here and he *will* run. He won't be able to handle it. A baby doesn't fit into his life. You know that. Hell the world knows that. He might as well be a rock star himself. I saw his beach house. That ain't someone that'll be there when things get tough. They don't stick it out. I may have screwed up but I won't run. I'll always be here."

I spun around. "He doesn't know okay. I'm not sure I'll even tell him. I don't want someone to save me. I can do this. I'm not helpless."

He started to open his mouth to argue when Granny Q walked into the room. I hadn't realized she was here.

"Stop begging her, Cain. You done made your bed boy, go lie in it. She moved on. Her heart has moved on. She's done shown us all she can go to school and take care of her sick momma and herself," she looked from Cain to me and a sad smile touched her lips. "Breaks my heart that you got another hurdle like this to walk through so young and this room is yours if you need it. But if you're set on leaving then I bless that too. You just be safe," she walked over and pulled me into a hug. "I love you like you're my own. Always have," she whispered into my hair.

Tears stung my eyes, "I love you too."

Granny Q pulled back and sniffed. "You keep in touch," she said and started to leave then glanced back at me. "Every man deserves to know he has a baby. Even if he ain't gonna be a part of its life he needs to know about it. You just keep that in mind."

She walked out of the room leaving Cain and I alone again. I put the last of my things in my suitcase and zipped it up. Grabbing the handle I picked it up. My nausea had gotten worse. I covered my mouth with one hand.

"Shit, B. You can't do that. Give it to me. You're not

supposed to pick up heavy stuff. See you can't do this. Who is gonna make sure you take care or yourself?"

The best friend I'd had all my life was back and the crazy boy who thought he was in love and ready to sacrifice his life was gone. "I told Bethy. She knows and I'm careful. I wasn't thinking. This is all new for me. And I think I'm gonna be sick."

"What can I do?" he asked with a panicked look on his face.

"Crackers would help."

Cain set the suitcase down and ran out of the room to get me crackers. He was back in less than a minute with a box of saltines and a glass. "Granny Q heard you. She already had the box out and a glass of ginger ale poured. She said the ale would soothe your stomach."

"Thank you," I replied and sat down on the bed to eat a cracker and sip on the ginger ale. Neither of us spoke. My nausea began to ease away and I had learned from experience to stop eating then. Too much and I'd be seeing it again very soon. Standing up I handed the box and glass back to Cain.

"Just put it down. I'll get it later," he picked up my suitcase. "Give me that box too. You can't carry it," he said shoving the box of things I hadn't unpacked from my last move under his arm. I pulled the last small bag up and he started for the door without another word. I followed him praying he didn't do something stupid when he saw Rush.

We got to the screen door leading out onto the front porch and he stopped, set the suitcase down and turned back around to look at me.

"You don't have to go with him. I told you that I could fix this. You have me, B. You've always had me."

Cain believed what he was saying. I could see it in his face. But I knew better. If I needed a friend, Cain would be there, but he was no one's savior. I didn't need one anyway. I had myself.

I pulled my bag up higher on my shoulder and thought carefully about how to explain this to him one more time. I'd tried everything. He wouldn't understand the truth. Bringing up how he had failed me when my mom was sick and I was so alone would only hurt him. "I need to do this."

Cain let out a frustrated growl and ran his hand through his hair. "You don't trust me to take care of you. That hurts so damn much." He let out a defeated laugh. "But then why should you? I let you down before. With your mom . . . I was a kid, B. How many times do I have to tell you that things are different now? I know what I want. I . . . God, B, I want you. It's always been you."

A lump formed in my throat. Not because I loved Cain, but because I did care for him. He was a big part of my life. He had been for as long as I could remember. I closed the distance between us and reached out and grabbed his hand. "Please, understand. This is something I have to do. I have to face this. Let me go."

Cain let out a weary sigh. "I'm always letting you go, B. You've asked that of me before. I keep trying but it's slowly destroying me."

One day he would thank me for leaving him. "I'm sorry, Cain. But I need to go. Rush's waiting on me."

Cain picked the suitcase back up and opened the screen door with his shoulder. Rush stepped out of the Rover as soon as he saw us. "Don't say anything to him, Cain." I whispered.

Cain nodded and I followed him down the steps. Rush met us at the bottom and looked up at me. "Is this all your stuff?" he asked.

"Yeah," I replied.

Cain didn't make a move to give him the suitcase and box. Rush's jaw ticked and I knew he was trying real hard to be good.

"Give him the stuff, Cain," I said from behind him nudging him in the back.

Cain sighed and handed the box and suitcase to Rush who took both items and headed for the Rover with them.

"You need to tell him," Cain muttered when he turned back around to look at me.

"I will, eventually. I need to think it through."

Cain looked past me toward my truck. "You leaving your truck?"

"I was hoping you could stick it up at the body shop and put a for sale sign on it. Maybe get a thousand out of it. Then you could keep half and send me the other half."

Cain frowned. "I'll sell the truck, B, but I ain't taking no money. I'll send it all."

I didn't argue with him. He needed to be able to do this and I'd let him. "Okay, fine. But could you give Granny Q some of it at least? For letting me stay here and all."

Cain's eyebrows shot up, "You want my Granny to ride her ass down to Rosemary to tan your hide?"

Smiling I closed the distance between us and holding onto his shoulders I stood on my tiptoes and placed a kiss on his cheek. "Thank you, for everything," I whispered.

"You can come back if you need me. Always," his voice cracked and I knew I needed to go. I stepped back and nodded once before walking back to the Rover.

Rush had the door open on the passenger side when I got there and he closed it behind me. I watched as he looked back at Cain before going and getting in on his side. I was really doing this. Letting go of what was safe and taking the first move in finding my place in the world.

RUSH

She looked like she was about to cry and I was afraid to ask her if she was okay. My fear that she may change her mind and stay in Sumit kept me quiet until we were safely out of the town limits. Glancing down at her hands knotted tightly in her lap bothered me. I wish she'd say something.

"You good?" I asked, unable to stop myself. My need to protect her took over.

She nodded, "Yeah. It's just a little scary I guess. This time I know I'm not coming back here. I also know I don't have a dad waiting to help me out. Leaving was harder this time."

"You got me," I replied.

She tilted her head to the side and looked at me. "Thank you. I needed to hear that right now."

Hell, I'd record it so she could replay it over and over if it would help. "Don't ever think you're alone."

She gave me a weak smile the turned her attention back to the road. "You know I could drive if you would like to sleep this time."

The idea of being free to look at her all I wanted was tempting. But she'd expect me to sleep and I wasn't wasting any time I had with her by sleeping through it. "I'm good. Thanks, though."

I'd gone through a drive-thru and gotten something to eat on the drive down here. She'd been sleeping and I hadn't wanted to disturb her, but she had to be hungry now.

"I'm starving. What sounds good to you?" I asked pulling back onto the interstate that would lead us back to Florida.

"Um . . . I . . . I don't know. Maybe soup."

Soup? That was an odd request. But, hell, if she wanted soup I'd get her some soup.

"Soup it is. I'll keep my eyes open for a restaurant."

"If you're starving please just stop wherever you want. I can find something to eat anywhere." She sounded nervous again.

"Blaire, I'm getting you soup," I replied glancing over at her with a smile.

"Thanks," she said and studied her hands in her lap again.

We didn't speak for a while. It felt good just to have her in the car with me. I didn't want her to feel like she had to talk.

We came to an exit with food and I pointed to the sign. "Looks like there are good options here. Pick a place," I told her.

She shrugged, "Doesn't matter. You know, if you don't want to get out and just stay on the road I could eat something car-friendly."

I wanted to draw this day out as long as I possibly could. "We're getting soup," I replied.

A small laugh startled me and I looked over to see her actually smiling. Making her do that more often was a new goal.

Blaire was asleep again when we pulled into the parking lot at Bethy's apartment later that night. I'd been careful to keep our conversation easy. After awhile we fell into a comfortable silence then she'd fallen asleep.

I put the Rover in park then sat back and looked at her. I'd glanced over at her sleeping a million times on the ride home. Just for a few minutes I wanted the freedom to watch her sleep. The dark circles under her eyes worried me. Was she not sleeping enough? Bethy might know. I could talk to her about it. Asking Blaire questions like that right now probably wasn't wise.

A soft knock on my window tore my attention from Blaire to Jace who was standing outside the car with an amused look on his face. I opened the door and stepped out before he could wake her up. I wanted to wake her up and I didn't want an audience when I did it.

"You planning on waking her up or you considering kidnapping?" Jace asked.

"Shut up, asshole."

Jace chuckled. "Bethy's anxious for Blaire to get back so she can hear about the trip. I'll help you with her stuff if you'll wake her up and get her inside."

"She's tired. Bethy can wait until tomorrow." I didn't want her to have to wakeup to a nosy Bethy. She obviously needed to sleep and she needed more food too. She'd barely eaten her soup earlier. I'd tried to stop for food again, but she'd said she wasn't hungry. That needed to change. It was like those damn peanut butter sandwiches all over again.

"Then you tell Bethy that," Jace replied, as I shoved the box in his hands and pulled the suitcase out of the back.

"I got the suitcase you take the box in and I'll wake her up."

"Private moment?" Jace smirked and I shoved the box a little too hard causing him to stumble back which only made him cackle with laughter.

I ignored him and walked over to the passenger side. Waking her up and letting her leave me wasn't exactly what I wanted to do. It scared the shit out of me. What if this was it? What if Blaire never let me near her like this again? No. I couldn't let that happen. I'd work slow but I would make sure this wasn't it for us. Although having had a full day of her all to myself was going to make it real hard to go back to the way it was.

I unbuckled her seatbelt. She barely stirred. A lock of hair had fallen in her face so I gave in to the urge to touch it. Reaching up I tucked the hair behind her ear. She was so damn beautiful. I'd never move on from her. It wasn't possible. I had to find a way to get her back. To help her heal.

Her eyelids fluttered open and her gaze locked with mine.

"We're here," I whispered not wanting to startle her.

She sat up and gave me a sheepish smile. "Sorry, I fell asleep on you again."

"You must have needed the rest. I didn't mind." I wanted to stay there and keep her in my car, but I couldn't do that. I moved back so she could get out. Asking her if I could see her tomorrow was right there on the tip of my tongue. But I didn't. She wasn't ready for that. I had to give her space. "I'll see you around then," I said and her smile wavered.

"Okay, uh, yeah, see you around. And thanks again for helping me today. I'll pay you back for the gas."

Like hell. "No you won't. I don't want your money. I was glad to help."

She started to say more but snapped her mouth shut. With a tight nod she turned and walked to the apartment.

BLAIRE

The first day back at work and Woods assigned me to the dining room. Breakfast and Lunch shifts. Not good. I stood outside the kitchen mentally preparing myself to not think about the smell. I'd woken up feeling queasy and forced two saltine crackers and some ginger ale down but that was all I could manage.

The moment I walked into the kitchen the smell would hit me. The bacon . . . oh, God, the bacon . . .

"You know you have to actually go in there sweet thing in order to work," Jimmy drawled from behind me. I spun around startled from my internal battle to see him smiling at me with an amused grin. "The cooks aren't that bad. You'll get over the yelling in no time. Besides last time you had them wrapped around your pretty little finger."

I forced a smile. "You're right. I can do this. I'm just not ready for people asking questions I guess." That wasn't exactly the truth but then it wasn't a lie either.

Jimmy opened the door and the smell slammed into me. Eggs, bacon, sausage, grease. Oh no. My body broke out into a cold sweat and my stomach rolled. "I, uh, need to use the restroom first," I explained and made my way to the employee restroom as fast as I could without breaking into a run. That would look even more suspicious.

I closed the door behind me and clicked the lock into place before falling to my knees on the cold tile and grabbing the toilet before everything I'd eaten last night and this morning came back out.

Several dry heaves later I stood up still feeling puny. I wet a paper towel to clean my face up. My white polo shirt was clinging to me from the sweat that had broken out all over me. I needed to change.

I rinsed my mouth with the mouthwash on the counter and straightened my shirt the best I could. Maybe no one would notice.

I could do this. I would just hold my breath while I was in the kitchen. That would do it. I'd breathe deeply before going in each time. I had to figure this out.

When I opened the door my eyes locked on Woods. He was standing against the wall facing the restroom with his arms crossed over his chest studying me. I was late.

"I'm sorry. I know I'm late. I just needed to take a quick break before I got started. I promise this won't happen again. I'll stay late to make up for it—"

"My office. Now," he snapped and turned to stalk down the hallway.

My heart sped up and I followed quickly behind him. I didn't want Woods to be mad at me. This job had been my answer for the next few months. Now that I'd talked myself into staying here and figuring out what to do I really didn't want to leave. Not yet.

Woods opened the door for me and I stepped inside.

"I really am sorry. Please don't fire me yet. I just—"

"I'm not firing you." Woods interrupted me.

Oh . . .

"Have you seen a doctor? I'm assuming it's Rush's. Does he know? Because if he does and you're here working for me in this condition I'm personally going to go break his fucking neck."

He knew. Oh no, oh no, oh no. I shook my head frantically. I had to stop this. Woods could not know. No one was supposed to know but Bethy. "I don't know what you're talking about."

Woods cocked an eyebrow. "Really?" the disbelief in his voice was unnerving. He wasn't going to fall for a lie. But I had a baby to protect.

"He doesn't know," the truth fell out of my mouth before I could stop it. "I don't want him to, yet. I need to find a way to do this on my own. We both know Rush doesn't want this. His family would hate it. I can't have my baby hated by anyone. Please understand," I begged.

Woods muttered a curse and ran his hands through his hair. "Rush deserves to know this, Blaire."

Yes he did. But when this baby had been conceived I'd not known just how sordid our worlds were. How impossible it would be for us to have a relationship. "They hate me. They hate my mom. I can't. Just, please give me time to prove I can do this without help. I'll tell him eventually, but I need to be stable and ready to leave after I do. This time my wants and his wants don't come first. I am doing what is best for this baby."

Woods frown deepened. We stood in silence for several minutes.

"I don't like it, but it isn't my story to tell. Go change and head out to see Darla. You can do cart rounds today. Let me know when the kitchen smell isn't so much of an issue."

I wanted to throw my arms around him and hug him. He wasn't forcing me to tell anyone and he was giving me an out on serving breakfast. I used to love bacon but now . . . I just couldn't deal with it. "Thank you. Dinner isn't bad. It's just the morning and sometimes the afternoons."

"Noted. I'll only put you on evening shifts in the dining room. This week you just work the course. But don't get overheated. Keep some ice or something to cool you down. Can I tell Darla?"

"No," I replied before he could finish. "She can't know. No one can know. Please."

Woods sighed then nodded his head. "Okay. I'll keep your secret. But if you need anything you'd better let me know . . . that is, if you're not going to let Rush know."

"Okay. Thank you."

Woods gave me a tight smile. "I'll see you later then."

I was dismissed.

The schedule for the rest of the week had me working the beer cart. There was a tournament a week from Saturday and I was down to work the entire day. I couldn't be happier about it. The money would be great. And although the heat was intense out on the course all day it was better than being in the air conditioning smelling bacon or any greasy meat and running off to vomit.

The club had gotten progressively busier since I'd left. According to Darla the members who only came during their summer vacations were all now in residence. Bethy and I ran two different carts in order to keep the place hydrated. Woods was rarely on the course so I didn't have to worry about his prying eyes. He was busy working. Jace had told Bethy that Woods was trying to prove to his dad that he was ready for a promotion.

After restocking my cart for the third time today, I headed back to the first hole to make my next round. I recognized the back of Grant's head right away. He was playing with . . . Nan. I'd known this day was coming but I hadn't been prepared for it. I could always skip this hole and let Bethy catch them on her next round but that would only be putting off the inevitable.

I pulled the cart up and Grant turned in my direction. He looked like he was in a serious conversation with Nan. The frustrated frown on his face wasn't comforting. He smiled but I could tell it was forced.

"We're good, Blaire. You can go on to the next hole," Grant called out. Nan's head jerked around at the sound of my name and the hateful scowl on her face had me shifting the cart in reverse. Maybe my first instincts had been right. I shouldn't have stopped.

"Wait. I want something." At the sound of Rush's voice my heart did a crazy little flutter thing that only he could make happen. I turned my head toward the sound of his voice to see him jogging toward me in a pair of pale blue shorts and a white polo shirt. It never ceased to amaze me that he could look so ridiculously good in such a preppy outfit. Boys in Bama did not dress like this for anything. They played golf in their jeans, baseball caps and whatever lucky t-shirt or flannel shirt made it out of the dryer that day. But Rush made it look like something mouthwateringly sexy.

"I need a drink," he said with an easy smile once he got to my cart. He stopped right in front of me. I hadn't seen him in a couple of days. Not since our road trip.

"The usual?" I asked stepping out of the cart only to be even closer to him. He didn't back up and our chests were close to brushing against each other. I glanced up at him.

"Yeah. That'd be great," he replied but didn't move. He also kept his eyes locked on mine. One of us was going to have to move and break this stare contest. I knew it should be me. I couldn't lead him to believe anything was different.

I scooted past him and walked to the back of the cart to get him a Corona. I bent down to pull one out of the ice and I felt him move in behind me. Dangit. He was not making this easy.

Standing up I didn't look back or turn around. He was too close. "What are you doing?" I asked quietly. I didn't want Nan or Grant to hear us.

"I miss you," was his simple response.

Closing my eyes tightly I took a deep breath and tried to calm the frenzy he was sending my heart into. I missed him too. But that didn't make the truth go away.

Telling him I missed him wasn't smart. I didn't need to let him believe things could go back to the way they were.

"Get your drink and come on," Nan snapped from behind him. That was enough to make me move. I wasn't up for a Nan verbal attack. Not today.

"Back off, Nan." Rush growled and I shoved the Corona at him and moved quickly back to the drivers seat. "Blaire, wait," Rush said once again following me.

"Don't do this," I begged. "I can't handle her."

He winced and then nodded before backing away. I tore my eyes off him and put the cart in drive without looking back I headed to the next hole.

RUSH

"Do you not remember what I asked you the other day, Nan?" I snarled once Blaire and her cart were out of sight.

"You were being pathetic. I was trying to help you not look like a love sick loser."

I turned around and stalked toward her. She was pushing me. I'd never had that all consuming rage most brothers have to physically harm their sisters when we were younger. But right now I was experiencing it.

Grant stepped in front of me putting a barrier between us. "Whoa. You need to back off and calm down."

I shifted my glare from Nan to Grant. What the fuck was he doing? He hated Nan. "Move. This is between me and *my* sister," I reminded him. He'd never claimed her before. Even when his father had been married to our mother he'd made sure we all understood he hated Nan. There had never been even a remote sibling attachment between those two.

"And you're gonna have to go through me to get to *your* sister," Grant replied taking a step in my direction. "'Cause right now you aren't thinking about anyone's feelings but Blaire's. Remember how Blaire's presence affects Nan. You cared about that once."

What the fuck! Was I sleeping? When did Grant start defending Nan? "I know exactly how Blaire affects Nan. But what I'm trying to get through to her is that nothing was Blaire's fault. She's hated the wrong person for so damn long she can't let go. What the hell is wrong with you anyway? You already knew this! You were the one who championed Blaire when she first showed up here. You never believed this was her fault. You saw her innocence in this from the beginning."

Grant shifted uncomfortably and then glanced back at Nan who's eyes had gone as round as saucers. "You made Nan weak, Rush. All her life you protected her. She relied on you. Then you go and drop her and focus all your attention on Blaire and expect her to be okay. She may be an adult but she has been so codependent on you her whole life she doesn't know any other way. If you weren't so damn focused on getting Blaire back you'd see that."

I shoved Grant out of my way and leveled my gaze on my sister. I didn't need this lecture from him even if there was some truth to it. Deep down I was pleased that these two had finally found a common ground. Maybe Grant cared for her after all. We had lived in the same house for years. We'd been neglected together.

"I love you, Nan. You know that. But you can't ask me to choose. It's not fair."

Nan put both her hands on her hips. It was her defiant position. "You can't love us both. I'll never accept her. She held a gun on me, Rush! You saw her. She's insane. She was going to shoot me. How can you love her *and* love me? That makes no sense."

"She would have never shot you. She held a gun on Grant too. He got over it. And yes I can love you both. I love you differently."

Nan shifted her gaze to Grant and gave him a sad smile. That was even weirder. "He won't listen to me, Grant. I give up. He is choosing his love for her over me and my feelings."

"Nan, just listen to him. Come on. He has a point," Grant told her in a gentle tone I'd never heard him use with her. I was in the fucking *Twilight Zone*.

Nan stomped her foot, "No! I hate her. I can't stand to look at her. She is hurting him now and I hate her more for it." Nan screamed. I glanced around to see if anyone had heard her and saw Woods walking toward us. *Shit*.

Grant turned and followed my gaze. "Ah, hell," he muttered.

Woods stopped in front of us and looked from Nan, to Grant and then to me. "I overheard enough to know what this conversation is about," he said keeping his focus locked on me. "Let me make myself very clear. We've all been friends most of our lives. I know the dynamic of your family," he shifted his gaze to Nan with a disgusted snarl of his lip then back to me. "If anyone has a problem with Blaire then they need to take it up with me. She has a job as long as she wants one. The three of you may not like it but I personally don't give a flying fuck. So get over it. She doesn't need this shit right now. Back off. Are we understood?"

I studied him. What did he mean and why was he acting as Blaire's protector? I didn't like it. My blood started to boil and I fisted my hands at my sides. Did he think he could make his move now? Show up when she was weak and be the hero? Hell no. That wasn't happening. Blaire was *mine*.

Woods didn't wait for a response. He stalked off instead.

"Looks like you have competition," Nan drawled.

Grant walked over to her and put her behind him again. "That's enough, Nan," he whispered then he looked over at me.

I was done with this. I couldn't deal with the two of them right now. I threw my club down and went after Woods.

He either heard me or felt the anger rolling off of me because he stopped just before he reached the clubhouse and turned around to look at me. One of his eyebrows shot up as if he were amused. That just pissed me off more.

"We both want the same thing. Why don't you take a few deep breaths and calm down?" Woods said as he crossed his arms over his chest.

"You stay away from her. Do you hear me? Back the fuck off. Blaire loves me she's just confused and hurt. She's also very vulnerable. So help me God if you so much as think you're going to take advantage of her current state I will beat the shit out of you."

Woods tilted his head to the side and frowned. He wasn't very affected by my warning. Maybe I needed to make him affected. "I know you love Blaire. I've never seen you act this crazed in your life. I get that. But Nan hates her. If you love her then protect her from the venom that is dripping from your sister's fangs. Or I will."

I felt like he'd slapped me in the face. Before I could respond Woods opened the door behind him and went inside. I stared at the closed door for several minutes before moving. I was going to lose one of them. I loved my sister, but over time I hoped she'd forgive me. I could lose Blaire forever. I wasn't going to allow that to happen.

BLAIRE

Bethy reached over and squeezed my hand. She was standing beside me as I sat on the doctor's table waiting. I'd peed in a cup and now we waited to hear the official results. My heart was racing. There was a slim possibility that I might not be pregnant. I had Googled it last night. The home pregnancy tests could have been wrong and I could have been getting sick because my head thought I was pregnant.

The door opened and a nurse walked in. She was smiling as she glanced from Bethy to me. "Congratulations. It's positive. You're pregnant."

Bethy's hand squeezed my tighter. I'd known this deep down but just hearing the nurse say it made it more real. I would not cry. My baby didn't need to know that I cried when I found out I was pregnant. I wanted him or her to always feel loved. This was not a bad thing. It could never be a bad thing. I needed family and I would soon have one again. Someone who loved me unconditionally.

"The doctor will be in to check things out in a few minutes. We need to do blood work too. Have you been experiencing any cramping or bleeding?"

"No. Just really sick. Smells set me off," I explained.

The nurse nodded and wrote that down on her clipboard. "It may not feel like it but that's a good thing. Being sick is good."

Bethy snorted. "You've not seen her dry heaving. Nothing's good about that."

The nurse smiled. "Yeah I can remember those days. That isn't fun," she shifted her gaze to me. "Will the father be involved?"

Would he? Could I tell him? I shook my head, "No, I don't think he will be."

The sad smile on the nurse's face as she nodded and made another note on her clipboard told me she saw this too often.

"Where you using any form of birth control when you conceived? The pill maybe?" the nurse asked.

I didn't look at Bethy. Maybe I didn't want her in here after all. I shook my head.

The nurse raised her eyebrows. "Nothing?" she asked.

"No, nothing. I mean we used a condom, but there was a couple times we didn't. He pulled out once . . . but once he didn't."

Bethy tensed beside me. I knew what she was thinking. How

could I have been so stupid? That had been one fact I'd left out of the story.

The nurse nodded. "Okay the doctor will be in shortly," she replied and stepped out of the room.

Bethy jerked on my arm causing me to look at her. "Rush didn't use a condom? Is he crazy? Dammit! He should've thought to ask you if you were pregnant. What a douche bag. Here I was feeling sorry for him because he doesn't know he's gonna be a papa and he didn't use a damn condom. He should have been contacting you in four weeks to make sure you *weren't* pregnant. What an *idiot*."

Bethy was pacing in front of me now. I just watched her. What did I say to this? I was just as wrong in the situation. I'd been the one to strip naked and climb on top of him and fuck his brains out that night. He'd been a guy and the last thing on his mind had been stopping to put on a condom. I hadn't given him much time to think. But sharing the details of mine and Rush's sex life with Bethy wasn't going to happen. So I kept my mouth shut.

"He deserves this. He should have checked on you. Don't tell the jackass. He thinks he can use that thing and not put a jacket on it then he can live in ignorance for all I care. I'll be here for you. Me and you. We got this," Bethy looked ready to take on the world at the moment. It made me smile. I wouldn't be in Rosemary when the baby was born. I wish I could be. I wanted my baby to have someone else to love it. Bethy would make an excellent aunt. The thought made me sad. My smile disappeared.

"I'm sorry. I didn't mean to upset you," Bethy said dropping her hands from her waist with a concerned look on her face.

"No. You didn't. I just wish . . . I just wish I didn't have to leave. I want my baby to know you."

Bethy walked over and wrapped her arms around my shoulders and squeezed. "You will tell me where you live and I'll come see the two of you all the time. Or you could stay and live with me. When the baby is born Rush is bound to be gone. He doesn't stay in Rosemary past the summer. We'd have time to get you two settled into life before he came back. Just think about it. Don't worry over any final decisions right now."

Would Rush give up on me and leave Rosemary? Or would he stay? My heart hurt thinking of him walking away from me. As badly as I knew it wouldn't work I wanted him to fight for me. I wanted him to find a way that we could be together, even if I knew it was impossible.

Two hours later we were back at Bethy's apartment and I had prenatal vitamins and several pamphlets about having a healthy pregnancy. I tucked them away in my room. I needed a warm bath and a nap.

Bethy knocked once on the bathroom door and walked inside. She was holding her phone in one hand and smiling like an idiot. "You're not going to believe this," she paused and shook her head like she was still in disbelief. "Woods just called. He said the condo is ours for the same cost I am paying now for this apartment. He said it's a job perk since having two of his employees on the club grounds will be helpful. He also said we would both be without a job if we tried to decline his offer."

I sank down onto the closed toilet seat and stared up at her. He was doing this because I was pregnant. This was his way of helping out. I wanted to scream at him and hug his neck all at one time. Tears stung my eyes. "Is he still on the phone?" I asked when I realized Bethy was still holding it close to her ear.

"No this is Jace. He said this has to do with you. You aren't . . . like seeing Woods or anything are you?" She asked slowly. That must have been Jace's question. She was repeating it like she didn't believe it even as she said it.

"Can you mute the phone?" I asked her quietly.

Her eyes went wide and she nodded. Once it was safely muted she stared at me like she didn't recognize me. What did she think? I was leading Woods on while I was pregnant with Rush's baby? Surely not. "Bethy, he knows. Woods knows."

Realization dawned on her and her mouth dropped open. "How?" she asked.

"He put me on the morning shift in the dining room. The kitchen . . . it smelled like bacon."

Bethy made a big "o" with her mouth and nodded. She got it. She reached up and unmuted her phone. "There is nothing going on with Woods and Blaire. He has just become a friend of hers and wants to help out. That's all."

Bethy rolled her eyes at something Jace said then called him crazy and hung up. "Okay, so Woods knows you're pregnant with Rush's baby and he's giving us a condo for dirt cheap? This is like the best thing ever. Wait until you see this place. If he lets us stay after the baby is born your room is plenty big enough for a crib! It's perfect."

I couldn't think that far ahead. Right now I just needed to go find Woods and talk to him. If I did leave in four months I didn't want this deal to go away for Bethy. I needed to make sure of that before I let her get too excited.

RUSH

Jace had called to let me know the girls were moving into the condo on the club property today. I hadn't seen Blaire since the incident on the golf course. Not for lack of trying. I'd tried to put myself in her path at the club several times and it never worked. I'd even stopped by yesterday and she'd been gone. Darla had said she and Bethy were both off work so I assumed they'd gone to do something together.

I pulled up to Bethy's apartment and instantly noticed Woods' car. What the hell was he doing here? I jerked my door open and headed for the door when I heard Blaire's voice. Turning I walked toward Woods' car until I saw him leaning against the wall it was parked beside and listening to Blaire with a smile on his face. One I was about to wipe off.

"If you're sure, then thank you," Blaire said quietly as if she didn't want anyone to hear her.

"Positive," Woods replied as his eyes lifted and met mine. The smile on his face disappeared.

Blaire turned her head to glance over her shoulder. The surprise on her face hurt. Maybe I shouldn't be here right now. I didn't want to lose it and scare her off and I was real close to going into a blind rage. Why were they alone talking? What was Woods positive about?

"Rush?" Blaire said walking away from Woods and toward me. "What are you doing here?"

Woods chuckled and shook his head then opened his car door. "I'm sure he came to help. I'll leave before he takes that ugly snarl out on me."

He was leaving. Good.

"Are you here to help us move?" She asked watching me carefully.

"Yeah, I am," I replied. The tension slowly leaving me as Woods BMW roared to life and drove off.

"How did you know we were moving?"

"Jace called me," I replied.

She shifted her feet nervously. I hated that I made her nervous.

"I wanted to help, Blaire. I'm sorry about Nan the other day. I've talked to her. She won't be—"

"Don't worry about it. You don't have to apologize for her. I don't hold it against you. I understand."

No she didn't. I could see it in her eyes that she didn't understand. I reached out and took her hand. I just needed to touch her somehow. She trembled as my fingers brushed her palm. Her teeth bit down on her bottom lip the same way I wanted to.

"Blaire," I said and stopped because I wasn't sure what else to say. The truth was too much right now.

She lifted her eyes from our hands and I could see the desire there. Really? Was I dreaming this one up or was she . . . was she really? I slipped a finger up her palm and caressed the inside of her wrist. She trembled again. Holy shit. She was affected by my touch. I stepped closer to her and ran my hand slowly up her arm waiting on the moment she pushed me off and put the distance between us I expected from her.

When I got high enough my thumb grazed the side of her breast and she reached out her hand and grabbed my free arm as she shuddered. What the fuck? "Blaire," I whispered pressing her back until she was against the brick wall of the apartment building and my chest was inches away from touching hers.

She didn't push me off and her eyelids looked heavy as she stared at my chest. Her breathing was heavy. The cleavage her little pale pink sundress showed off was right there under my nose. Rising and falling as if it was an invitation. An impossible one. Something was off here.

I put my other hand on her waist and slowly slid it up her body until my other thumb was tucked under her breast. She wasn't wearing a bra. Her nipples were hard and erect poking against the thin material of her dress. I couldn't stop myself. I eased my hand up and covered her right breasts squeezing it gently. Blaire whimpered and her knees started to give out. She let her head fall back on the wall and closed her eyes. I held her steady and slipped my leg between hers to keep her from sinking to the ground.

With my other hand I covered her left breast and ran the pads of my thumbs over her firm nipples.

"Oh God, Rush," she moaned opening her eyes and staring at me through her lowered lashes. Holy fuck. I was in some form of tortured heaven. If this was another dream I was going to be pissed. It felt too real.

"Does that feel good, baby?" I asked, lowering my head to whisper in her ear.

"Yes," she breathed sinking down further onto my knee. When her warm center pressed against my leg she gasped and gripped my arms harder. "Ahhhh," she cried out.

I was going to come in my pants. I'd never been this turned on in my life. Something was different. This wasn't the same. She was almost desperate. I could sense her fear but her need was stronger. "Blaire, tell me what you want me to do. I'll do whatever it is you need," I promised, kissing the soft skin under her ear. She smelled so damn good. I kneaded her breasts in my hands again and she let out a pleading whimper. My sweet Blaire was incredibly horny. This was real. This wasn't a damn dream. Holy fuck.

"Blaire!" the shrill call of Bethy's voice was like a bucket of ice water thrown over Blaire. She stiffened, then stood up dropping her hands from me and scooted away. She couldn't look at me.

"I . . . uh . . . I'm sorry. I don't know . . ." She shook her head and hurried away from me. I watched until she was at the door and Bethy was talking to her sternly. Blaire was nodding. Once they went inside I slammed both hands against the brick and muttered a string of curses while I attempted like hell to get my raging hard on under control.

After a few minutes the door opened again and I turned to see Jace walking out. He looked over at me and let out a low whistle. "Damn man you work fast."

I didn't even respond to that. He didn't know what he was talking about. Blaire had been hungry for my touch. She hadn't pushed me away. She'd been almost begging me silently. It made no sense, but she'd wanted me. God knows I wanted her. I always wanted her.

"Come on. We have a couch to move. I need your help," Jace said holding the door open.

BLAIRE

What was wrong with me? I walked back into Bethy's bedroom and closed the door. I needed a minute to calm down. I'd been ready to beg Rush to screw me right there. It was that stupid dream. Okay maybe last night's dream hadn't been stupid but it had been extremely intense. Thinking about it had me squeezing my legs together.

Why was I doing this now? Sexual dreams were one thing but now they were vivid and so real I was basically orgasming in my sleep. It was insane. Not once in Sumit had I been this horny. But then Rush hadn't been in Sumit.

I sank down onto the bare mattress that Bethy had stripped for the move. I had to pull myself together around him. He hadn't been trying to come on to me but I'd been a panting wild woman from the moment his fingers touched my hand. How embarrassing. Facing him after that was going to be hard.

The door opened and Bethy walked in with a small grin on her face. Why was she grinning now? She'd jumped all over me when she'd caught me outside. "Your pregnancy hormones are kicking in," she said after the door behind her was firmly closed.

"What?" I asked confused.

Bethy cocked her to head to the side, "Have you not read any of those pamphlets the doctor sent home with you? I'm sure one of them tells you about this."

I was still confused. "About the fact I can't control myself around Rush?"

Bethy shrugged, "Yeah. I guess he'd be the one that did it for you. But you get horny while pregnant, Blaire. I know this because my cousin used to make jokes about his wife when she was pregnant. Said he had a hard time keeping up with her and all."

Horny? Pregnancy was making me horny? Just great.

"Probably only gonna be an issue with Rush. I figure he's the only person you are attracted to and want that way. So it's just gonna be more intense around him. Maybe you should tell him and enjoy this. I have no doubt he'd help out."

I couldn't tell him. Not yet. I wasn't ready and neither was he. Nan would be furious and I couldn't handle that right now. Besides, Rush would choose Nan and I couldn't handle that happening again either. "No. He doesn't need to know. Not right now. I'll be better."

Bethy shrugged, "Fine. I said my piece. You don't wanna tell him then don't but when you crack and fuck his brains out could you not do it in public?" She asked with a smirk then opened the door and walked back out.

"You need to wrap it up in a quilt first! You're gonna ruin my cushions," Bethy yelled at the guys.

I could face him. He didn't know about this. I would act like nothing happened. Besides I needed to help do something. I could finish packing up the kitchen.

Rush was watching me. Every time he came back into the apartment to move something else his eyes found me. I'd dropped a bowl, spilled a box of cereal and dumped out a box of flatware because of those heated looks. How was I supposed to concentrate and not be a clumsy idiot with him looking at me like that?

When he walked back into the apartment this time I decided I'd go pack things up in the bathroom instead. They would be moving the kitchen table and chairs next and I'd probably break every glass Bethy had.

I stepped into the bathroom and suddenly there was a body behind me moving me in further. The heat from Rush's chest pressing against my back made me shiver. Dangit. I wasn't going to be able to handle this.

The bathroom door closed and the familiar sound of the lock clicking into place only made my heart beat faster. He wanted more of what had happened outside and I was so worked up by being near him I wasn't going to be able to think straight.

Rush's hand brushed the hair on my neck away and he moved it over my shoulder. When the warmth of his lips touched my bare skin I may have whimpered. Both of his hands rested on my hips and he pulled me back against him even more. "You're driving me crazy, Blaire. Insane, baby. Fucking insane." He whispered against my ear. It took all my willpower not to let my head fall back on his chest. "What was that outside? You had me so damn worked up. All I can see is you."

His hands moved up my sides then moved over my stomach. The almost protective placement of them, even though he had no idea what he was protecting made me tear up. I wanted him to know. But I also wanted him to choose me . . . and our baby. I didn't think he could do that. He loved his sister. I was terrified of that kind of rejection and I refused to let my baby be rejected.

I started to move out of his embrace when his hands moved up to cup my breasts and his mouth began nibbling on the curve of my neck. Oh, hell. I might not trust him with my heart, but I really wanted to trust him with my body. Even if it was just this once.

"What're you doing?" I asked breathlessly.

"Praying to God you won't stop me. I'm a starving man, Blaire." He paused waiting on me to reply. When I didn't he reached up and pulled the straps of my sundress down until my breasts were bare. They felt swollen all the time now and it made them so sensitive. I was going without a bra more and more. My bra didn't exactly fit anymore and I hadn't wanted to spend money on a new one if this bigger boobs thing didn't last long.

"Damn, baby. They look bigger," he said as his hands covered them.

Wetness instantly pooled in my panties and my knees went weak. I grabbed the wall for support. Nothing had ever felt this good. A needy sound came out of my mouth, but I wasn't sure what it was.

Suddenly I was being picked up and spun around. Then my bottom was put on the counter, before Rush's mouth covered mine and his hands went right back to my breasts. I wasn't going to be able to stop this. I wanted it like I wanted my next breath. I had never needed sex of any kind before but this was something I couldn't control.

Rush's kiss was wild and as out of control hungry as I felt. He bit down on my bottom lip and pulled my tongue into his mouth and sucked. Then his hand tugged on my nipples and I lost it. I needed his shirt off now. Grabbing at it I pulled until he stepped back a fraction and jerked it over his head, then he was devouring my mouth again.

His hands were doing delicious things to my breasts and I couldn't get him close enough.

A knock sounded at the door and Rush pulled me up against his chest. I shuddered and closed my eyes from the pleasure. He turned his head toward the door. "Go the fuck away," he snarled at whoever was out there.

A smothered laugh was all we heard, before Rush was kissing a trail down my neck and across my collarbone until his mouth hovered over my right nipple. The heat from his breath made me tremble and I grabbed his hair and forced his head closer with my silent plea. He chuckled then pulled my nipple into his mouth and began to suck. The wetness in my legs caught on fire or at least it felt like it did. If he hadn't been holding me down with his body I might have shot through the ceiling.

"Oh, God!" I screamed not caring if anyone heard me just needing this. My reaction made Rush greedier. He moved to my other nipple and began giving it the same treatment as his hand moved up the inside of my thigh. The idea that he was about to touch my very swollen wet area made me scared and excited at the same time. He'd know something wouldn't he? Could he tell I was different down there too? Then his fingers ran along the outside of my panties and I just didn't care anymore.

"Fuck. You're soaking wet," he groaned, and buried his head in my neck. His breathing was hard and erratic. "So wet." His fingers slipped inside of the crotch of my panties and into my swollen folds causing fireworks to ignite in my body.

I grabbed onto Rush's shoulders. My nails were digging into his skin but I couldn't help it. He was touching me. His mouth moved to my ear as he kissed me and his heavy breathing tickled my skin. "Such a sweet pussy. It's my pussy, Blaire. It'll always be mine." His naughty words as his finger slid in and out of me sent me close to the edge again.

"Rush, please," I begged clawing at him.

"Please what? You want me to kiss that sweet pussy?

'Cause it feels so damn hot and needy I need a taste." He was pulling my panties off and I was lifting my butt to allow him to. Then he pulled my dress up and I raised my hands to let him remove it.

"Sit back," he ordered moving me himself until my back touched the wall. Then he took both of my legs and bent them up until my feet were on the counter and I was wide open to him. "Damn, that's the hottest thing I've ever seen in my life," he whispered before dropping to his knees and covering me with his mouth. The first lick if his tongue and I was coming again.

"Oh, God, Rush please. Oh, God, Ahhhhh," I cried out as I held his head unable to let him stop. It was too good. The flick of his tongue over my clit was incredible. I needed more. I never wanted this to end. His finger slid through my opening then held it open as he licked and kissed me there.

"Mine. It's mine. You can't leave me again. I need this. You smell so fucking perfect. Nothing is ever going to be this damn perfect for me," he murmured, as he tasted me. I was ready to agree to anything he wanted.

"I need in you," he said lifting his eyes to look up at me. I just nodded.

"I don't have a condom," he paused and closed his eyes tightly, "but I'll pull out."

It didn't matter now. But I couldn't tell him that. I just nodded again.

Rush was up with his jeans down instantly. He grabbed my

hips and moved me back to the edge of the counter until the head of his erection was touching me. The question in his eyes was unmistakable even if he didn't say it aloud. I reached down and took his erection and guided it inside me.

"Fuck," he moaned as he pressed the rest of the way until I was full. Completely full of Rush.

I wrapped my arms around his neck and held him. For just a second I needed to hold him. This wasn't about my crazy hormones anymore. Now that he was in me I felt home. Complete and I was about to cry. Before I could embarrass myself and confuse him I lifted my head and whispered in his ear. "Fuck me."

It was as if I'd pulled the trigger on a loaded gun. Rush grabbed my hips with both his hands and let out a growl before pumping in and out of me. The climb toward the spiral I knew was going to come started up again and I rode him. Enjoying his moment of surrender and the complete abandon on his face as he brought us closer and closer to the climax we needed.

"I love you, Blaire. I love you so damn much it hurts," he panted then lowered his head to suck on my nipple. My body went off and I cried out his name. Rush lifted his head and looking into my eyes started to pull out and I clamped my legs around his waist. I didn't want him to pull out. The understanding of what I wanted hit him and he said my name on a whisper before throwing his head back as he pumped his release into me.

RUSH

Blaire pushed me back and jumped down off the counter before I could get my head clear from that orgasm. "Wait, I need to clean you up," I told her. I actually wanted to clean her up. I liked it. No, I fucking loved it. Knowing I'd been there and I was taking care of her did something to me.

"You don't need to clean me up. I'm fine," Blaire replied as she reached for her discarded dress and slipped it back on without making eye contact with me. Shit. Had I read her wrong? I thought she wanted this. No. I *knew* she wanted it. She'd been so damn hungry for it.

"Blaire, look at me."

She paused and picked up her panties. I swallowed hard as she stepped into them and slid them back up her body. I needed her again. She couldn't walk away from me now. I wasn't going to be able to live through it if she did.

"Blaire, please look at me," I begged.

Stopping, she took a deep breath then lifted her eyes to meet mine. The sadness there was mixed with something else. Embarrassment? Surely not. I reached over and cupped her face with my hand. "What's wrong? Did I do something you didn't want me to? Because I was trying to not lose control. I was trying real hard to do what you wanted."

"No. You . . . you didn't do anything wrong." She dropped her eyes from mine again. "I just need to think. I need some space. I didn't . . . I wasn't . . . We shouldn't have done that."

Stabbing me in the chest would have been less painful. I wanted to pull her to me and go all cave man claiming she was mine and couldn't leave me. But then I might lose her and I couldn't go through that again. I had to do this her way. I let my hand fall from her face and I stepped back so she could leave.

Blaire lifted her face to look up at me again. "I'm sorry," she whispered then opened the door and escaped.

She had just blown my world away with amazing hot sex and she was sorry. Fantastic.

When I finally emerged from the bathroom Blaire was gone. Jace smirked and Bethy made excuses for her. I didn't want to be there anymore either. After I made sure all the heavy stuff was moved and Blaire's suitcase and box were packed up I left. I couldn't stay there while the two of them watched me. They'd heard us. Blaire had been loud. I wasn't ashamed, I was just tired of them looking at me and waiting on me to say something to explain Blaire's departure.

* * *

I gave Blaire a couple days to come to me. She didn't. I wasn't surprised. She'd asked for space and I'd given her all the space I could handle. I decided to got to the club and play a round of golf. I was sure to see here there. I didn't call anyone to play with me, I didn't want anyone around when Blaire showed up. We needed to talk. No distractions or excuses for her to ride off.

It had sounded like a firm plan but after six holes and no cart girl I was beginning to wonder. Just as I was about to walk to the next hole I heard the sound of the cart. I stopped and turned around. The blood that had started pumping through my veins from the idea of seeing Blaire out here and having her alone froze when I realized it was that blond girl that I'd seen a few times training with Bethy. Shit.

I shook my head and waved her on. I didn't want a drink from her. She smiled brightly and drove on to the next stop.

"It's hot out here. You sure you don't want something?" Meg's voice asked and I glanced back to see her walking up dressed in a white tennis skirt and polo. She'd been big into tennis ten years ago too.

"Wrong cart girl," I replied and waited on her to catch up to me.

"You only buy from one?"

"Yep."

Meg looked thoughtful then nodded, "I see. You have a thing for a cart girl."

"A thing" didn't even scratch the surface. I pulled my golf bag up on my shoulder and started walking to the next hole. I wasn't going to respond to that comment.

"And he's touchy about it," Meg quipped. That annoyed me.

"Or it's just not your business."

She let out a low whistle. "So it's more than a thing."

I stopped and leveled my gaze on her. Just because she was my first fuck didn't mean we had any kind of bond or friendship. This was pissing me off. "Let it go." I warned.

Meg put her hands on her hips and her jaw fell open. "Oh my god . . . Rush Finlay has fallen in love. Holy shit! I never thought I'd see the day."

"You haven't seen me in ten years, Meg. How the hell do you know anything about me?" The annoyed snarl in my voice didn't even make her flinch.

"Listen, Finlay. Just because you haven't seen me in ten years doesn't mean I haven't seen or heard about you. I've been back in town several times, but you were always partying it up at casa de Finlay and screwing every model-perfect body that came your way. I didn't see a point in showing back up in your life. But yeah, I've seen you and like the rest of this town I know that you're a rich, gorgeous player who can have his pick of the litter."

I didn't like the picture she painted of me. I sounded shallow. Did Blaire see me that way? Not only could she not trust me to choose her and protect her, but did she think I'd just move on when someone else came along too? Surely she knew that wasn't true.

"She's amazing. No . . . she's perfect. Everything about her is fucking perfect," I said aloud then shifted my gaze back to Meg.

"I don't just love her, she owns me. Completely. I'd do anything for her."

"But she doesn't feel the same way?" Meg asked.

"I hurt her. Not the way you're thinking either. The way I hurt her is hard to explain. There is so much pain in what happened that I don't know if I can ever get her back."

"Is she a cart girl?"

She was really hung up on the cart girl thing. "Yeah she is." I paused and wondered if I should tell her exactly who Blaire was. Saying it aloud to someone and admitting this might help me make sense of it. "She and Nan have the same father." I hadn't meant to say it like that.

"Shit," Meg muttered. "Please tell me she's nothing like your evil little sister."

Nan had very few fans. I didn't even flinch at the accusation that she was evil. She'd brought this on herself. "No. She's nothing like Nan."

Meg was quiet a moment and I wondered if this was as far as this conversation was going to go. Then she shifted her feet and pointed back toward the club house. "Why don't we go have some lunch and you can tell me all about this very strange situation and I'll see if I can't come up with some wisdom or at the very least female advice."

I needed any advice I could get. There were no females in my life I could ask for help. "Yeah, okay. Sounds good. You give me any advice I can use and lunch is on me."

BLAIRE

This was the second day that I had woken up without getting sick. I'd even had Bethy cook bacon to test me out before I came in for the lunch shift. I figured if I could survive the smell of bacon then I could do this. My stomach had rolled and I'd gotten nauseous but I hadn't thrown up. I was getting better.

I called Woods and assured him I would be fine to work in the dining room. He told me to come on in they were short staffed and he needed me. Jimmy was standing in the kitchen grinning when I walked in thirty minutes before the lunch shift.

"There's my girl. Glad that stomach virus has gone. You look like you lost ten pounds. How long were you sick?" Woods had told Jimmy and anyone else who asked that I had a virus and I was recovering. I'd only worked two shifts on the course and I never ran into kitchen staff while on the carts.

"I probably lost some weight. I'm sure I'll gain it back soon enough," I replied and hugged him.

"You better or I'm shoving donuts down your throat until I can wrap my hands around your waist and my fingers not touch."

That may be sooner than he realized I thought. "I could use a good donut right now."

"It's a date. After work. You, me and a twelve pack. Half chocolate covered," Jimmy said and handed me my apron.

"Sounds good. You can come see my new place. I'm staying with Bethy in a condo on the club property."

Jimmy's eyebrows shot up. "You don't say. Well, well, well aren't you highfalutin."

I tied my apron on and tucked my pen and pad in my front pocket. "I'll take the first round if you prep the salads and make the sweet tea."

Jimmy winked. "Deal."

I headed out to the dining room and luckily the only guests were two older gentlemen I'd seen before but I didn't know their names. I took down their orders and poured them both a cup of coffee before heading back to check on the salads.

Jimmy had two already made for me and was holding them up when I walked back into the kitchen. "Here ya go, hot stuff," he said.

"Thanks, gorgeous," I replied and took the salads and headed back into the dining room. I delivered the salads and took the drink order of new guests and headed back to get their sparkling water and spring water with lemon. No one ever just ordered water around here.

Jimmy was heading out the kitchen door when I got there. "I just got the two women who look like they came off the tennis courts. I think I saw Hillary . . . isn't that the hostess today? Anyway I think I saw her talking to more guests so there should be a table waiting to be greeted."

He saluted me and headed back to the dining room.

I quickly finished getting the special waters and put the two orders of crab bisque the men had requested onto my tray then headed back to the dining room when Jimmy's panicked expression caught my attention.

"I got this," he said reaching for my tray.

"You don't even know where it goes. I can carry a tray Jimmy," I replied rolling my eyes. He didn't even know I was pregnant and he was being silly . . .

Then I saw him or them. Jimmy wasn't being silly. He was protecting me. Rush's head was tilted forward as he talked about something that caused that intense serious expression on his face. The woman had long dark hair. She was gorgeous. Her cheekbones were high and perfect. Long heavy lashes outlined her dark eyes. I was going to be sick. My tray rattled and Jimmy was taking it from me. I let him. I was about to drop it.

He wasn't mine. But . . . I was carrying his baby. He didn't know. But he'd made love to me, no, he'd fucked me in Bethy's bathroom just three days ago. This hurt. So bad. I swallowed. My throat almost felt closed. Jimmy was saying something to me, but I couldn't understand him. I was unable to do anything except stare at them. Rush leaned in close to her, like he didn't want anyone to hear what he was saying.

Her eyes shifted from Rush's and they locked with mine. I hated her. She was beautiful and refined and everything I wasn't. She was a woman. I was a girl. A pathetic girl who needed to get the hell out of here and stop making a scene. Even if it was a silent scene I was still just standing frozen staring at them. She studied me and a small frown creased her forehead. I didn't want her asking Rush about me and pointing me out. I spun around and fled the dining room.

As soon as I was out of the guests view, I broke into a run and ran right into Woods's hard chest. "Whoa . . . there, sweetheart. Where are you running off to? Still too much for you?" He asked sticking his finger under my chin and tilting my head up so he could see my face.

I shook my head and a tear escaped. I was not going to cry about this dammit. I'd asked for it. I'd pushed him away. I'd walked out on him after the amazing sex. What did I expect? That he'd sit around pinning for me. Hardly. "I'm sorry, Woods. Just give me a minute and I'll be fine. I promise you. I just need a moment to get myself together."

He nodded and ran a hand up and down my arm in a comforting way. "Is Rush in there?" he asked almost hesitantly.

"Yeah," I choked out forcing the tears filling my eyes to go away. I took a deep breath and blinked them away. I wasn't going to do this. I was going to control my crazy emotions.

"Is he with someone?" Woods asked.

I just nodded. I didn't want to say it.

"You want to go to my office and chill out a bit. Wait until they're gone?"

Yes. I wanted to go hide from this, but I couldn't. I had to learn to live with it. Rush would be in Rosemary for another month. I had to learn to deal. "I can do this. It was just a surprise. That's all."

Woods lifted his gaze from mine and a cold expression came over his face. "Go away. This is not what she needs right now," Woods said in a hard angry tone.

"Get your motherfucking hands off her," Rush replied.

I stepped back away from Woods embrace and kept my eyes down. I didn't want to see Rush but I also didn't want him and Woods fighting either. Woods looked ready to fight for my honor. I had no idea how Rush looked because I wasn't going to check and see.

"I'm fine, Woods. Thank you. I'll get back to work," I mumbled and started to head back to the kitchen.

"Blaire, don't. Talk to me," Rush pleaded.

"You've done enough. Leave her the hell alone, Rush. She doesn't need this from you. Not now," Woods barked.

"You don't know anything," Rush growled and Woods took a step in Rush's direction. Woods was either going to blurt out that I was pregnant and make it very obvious that he did know something or he was going to start throwing punches with Rush. It was once again time for me to get over myself and fix it.

I turned back and went to stand in front of Rush. I looked up at Woods. "It's okay. Just give me a minute with him. It'll be okay. He didn't do anything wrong. I was just being emotional. That's all," I told him.

Woods jaw worked back and forth as he grinded his teeth. Keeping his mouth shut was proving difficult for him. He finally nodded and stalked away.

I had to face Rush now.

"Blaire," Rush said gently as his hand reached out and grabbed mine. "Please look at me."

I could do this. I had to do this. I turned around letting Rush continue holding my hand in his. I should remove it, but I couldn't just yet. I'd seen him with a woman who was probably keeping his bed warm at night while I continued to push him away. I was losing him. So was our baby. But then . . . had we ever really had him?

I lifted my eyes and met his worried gaze. He didn't like upsetting me. I loved that about him. "It's okay. I overreacted. I was just, um, surprised is all. I should have known you'd have moved on by now. I just—"

"Stop it," Rush interrupted me and pulled me up against him. "I haven't moved anywhere. What you think you saw you didn't. Meg is an old friend. That is all. She means nothing to me. I came looking for you. I needed to see you and I went to play golf. You weren't there. I ran into Meg and she suggested we have lunch. That's it. I had no idea you were in here working. I'd have never done that. Even though I wasn't doing anything. I love you Blaire. Just you. I'm not with anyone else. I never will be."

I wanted to believe him. As selfish and wrong as it was I wanted to believe he loved me enough not to need anyone else. Even if I was pushing him away. But I was lying to him and he would hate me if I didn't tell him soon. I didn't want him to hate me. But I couldn't trust him. Did lying make that okay? Was lying ever okay?

"I'm pregnant." The words came out of me before I realized what I was doing. I covered my mouth in horror as Rush's eyes went wide. Then I turned and ran like hell.

RUSH

My feet were cemented to the floor. Even as I watched Blaire running away from me I couldn't move. Had I just dreamed that? Was it a desperate hallucination? Was I getting that bad?

"If you aren't going after her I am," Woods voice broke into my thoughts and I snapped out of my shocked haze.

"What?" I asked glaring at him. I hated him. Beating his face in was something I was suddenly fantasizing about.

"I said if you aren't going after her I am. She needs someone right now. As much as I don't want it to be you, because I don't think you deserve her, it needs to be you."

Did Woods know she was pregnant? My blood started to boil. Had Blaire told him she was pregnant but not me?

"I was here the first morning she tried to work and the smell of bacon sent her scrambling to the restroom to vomit. So, yeah I already knew. Get that crazed possessive gleam out of your eyes and go get her," Woods tone was laced with disgust.

"She's been sick?" My chest hurt. She'd been sick alone. I'd left her alone and she'd been suffering. Air wasn't getting to my lungs.

"Yeah, you stupid shit, she's been sick. That happens in her situation. But she's getting better. Now I'm about to turn and go after her. Make your move." Woods warned.

I broke into a run.

It wasn't until I exited the building in the back and looked up the hill that I found her. She was running toward the condos. She was going back to her place. I went after her. She was pregnant. Should she be running like this? What if it was bad for the baby? She needed to slow down.

"Blaire, stop. Wait," I called out when I was close enough. She slowed down and finally stopped as I caught up with her.

"I'm sorry," she sobbed with her face in her hands.

"What are you sorry for?" I asked, closing the distance between us and pulling her against me. I wasn't worried about scaring her off anymore. I wasn't letting her go anywhere.

"This. Everything. My being pregnant." She whispered stiff in my arms.

She was sorry. No. She wasn't going to be sorry for that. "You have nothing to be sorry for. Don't ever apologize to me again. Do you hear me?"

Some of the tension in her body eased and she leaned against me. "But I didn't tell you."

No she hadn't, but I understood. It sucked, but I understood. "I wish you had. I'd have taken care of you. I'm going to take care of you now. I'll make up for it. I swear."

Blaire shook her head and pushed back away from me. "No. I can't. We can't do this. I didn't tell you for a reason. We . . . we need to talk."

I was taking care of her and she wasn't leaving me. But if she needed to talk about it then I'd let her. "Okay. Let's go to your place since we're so close."

Blaire nodded and turned to walk toward the condo. Jace had said Woods was letting them stay there for the same amount as Bethy's old apartment. He thought Woods was thinking as using it as a tax write-off or something. I understood now. He'd been doing it for Blaire. He'd been taking care of her. Not anymore he wasn't. I'd go talk to Woods later, but I'd be paying the prime amount for rent on this place. Woods was not taking care of Blaire. She was mine.

I watched as she bent down and got the key from under the mat. That had to be the worst hiding spot ever for a key. I'd deal with that later too. I wasn't going to be able to sleep at night knowing she had a key tucked under her front door mat for anyone to walk in on her.

Blaire opened the door and stepped back. "Come on in."

I stepped inside and took her hand with me as I passed her. She may want to tell me all the reasons we couldn't be together but I was going to be touching her while she talked. I needed to know she was okay. Touching her calmed me down.

She closed the door and let me pull her over to the sofa. I sat down and pulled her down beside me. I wanted to put her in my lap but the worried nervous look on her face stopped me. She needed to talk and I was going to let her.

"I should have told you. I'm sorry I didn't. I was going to, maybe not the way I did today, but I was going to tell you. I just needed time to decide on what I was going to do with my life. I wanted to save up and go start somewhere new. For the baby. But I was going to tell you."

She was going to tell me then leave me? Panic gripped me. She couldn't do that. "You can't leave me," I said as plainly as I could. She needed to understand that.

Blaire dropped her gaze from mine and studied our hands. I'd laced my finger through hers. It was all that was keeping me calm at the moment. "Rush," she said softly. "I don't want my baby to ever feel unwanted. Your family . . ." she trailed off and her face had gone pale.

"My family will accept what I tell them to accept. If they don't I will take you and my baby and leave them to pay all their own damn bills. You come first, Blaire."

She shook her head and tugged her hand loose from mine and stood up. "No. You say that now, but it isn't true. It wasn't true a month ago and it isn't true now. You will always choose them over me. Or at least you will choose Nan and that's okay. I understand, I just can't live with it. I can't stay here."

Not telling her about her dad was going to haunt me for the

rest of my life. My need to protect Nan had fucked up the only thing important to me. I stood up and walked toward Blaire as she backed up until she was up against the wall. "No. One. Comes. Before. You."

Her eyes shimmered with unshed tears and she shook her head. I hated that she couldn't believe me.

"I love you. When you walked into my life I didn't know you. Nan was my first priority. But you changed that. You changed everything. I was going to tell you but my mom came home too soon. I was so scared to death of losing you that I lost you anyway. Nothing is going to take you away from me again. I'll spend the rest of my life proving to you that I love you. You and this baby," I touched her flat stomach and she trembled. "You come first."

"I want to believe you," she said through a sob.

"Let me prove it to you. Leaving me doesn't let me prove anything. You have to stay with me, Blaire. You have to give me a chance."

A tear slipped free and rolled down her face. "I'm gonna get big and fat. Babies cry all night and they cost money. I won't be the same. We won't be the same. You'll regret it."

She really didn't have a clue. No matter how many times I told her she didn't believe me. She'd lost everyone in her life she'd loved and trusted. Why should she believe me? The only man in her life had left her. Betrayed her. She expected nothing less.

"This baby brought you back to me. It's a part of us. I will never regret it. And you can get as big as a whale, I'll love you anyway."

A small smile tugged on her lips. "I better not get as big as a whale."

I shrugged, "Doesn't matter."

Her small smile quickly left. "Your sister. She's going to hate this. Me. The baby."

I would deal with Nan. If she couldn't cope then I'd take Blaire and we'd go somewhere far away. Blaire had been upset enough. I wasn't letting anyone else hurt her. "Trust me to protect you and put you first."

Blaire closed her eyes and then nodded.

My chest swelled and I wanted to shout to the world that this woman was mine. But instead I picked her up. "Where's your bedroom?" I asked.

"The last room on the left."

I walked back there. I wouldn't make love to her right now but I needed to hold her for a while. I pushed the door open and I froze. The bedroom was a nice size for a condo but the blanket on the floor with a single pillow was just one more strike against me. When I'd moved them I had known Blaire didn't have a bed. She'd been sleeping on the couch. But I had been so wrapped up in getting her back I hadn't thought about her needing a bed.

"I haven't got a bed yet," Blaire mumbled trying to get down out of my arms. I wasn't letting her go. I held her tighter against me. She'd slept on the hard ground last night while I'd been sleeping in my big king size bed. *Fuck*.

"You're shaking, Rush. Put me down," Blaire said tugging on my arm.

I spun around and stalked back to the living room then out of the door. Slamming the door behind me, I locked it and stuck the key in my pocket. I wasn't sticking it back under that damn mat.

"What are you doing?" Blaire asked.

My car wasn't here. I'd just have to carry her back down the hill and to my Rover. "I'm taking you to get a bed. A big ass bed. One that costs a fucking fortune," I growled. I was furious that I'd missed that one major issue. It was no wonder Woods had been taking care of her. I'd failed. I wasn't going to fail her again. I'd make sure she had it all.

"I don't need an expensive bed. I'm going to get a bed soon."

"Yeah, real soon. Tonight," I replied then bent my head and kissed her nose. "Let me do this. I need to do this. I need you tucked into the best bed money can buy. Okay."

A small smile tugged at her lips, "Okay."

BLAIRE

I didn't require more than a full size bed. However, Rush refused to get anything less than a king size bed, two bedside tables and a matching dresser with a gorgeous mirror. I made the mistake of looking too long at a pretty lavender quilt and matching shams. Before I knew what was happening he was buying the entire bed set complete with sheets and new pillows. I argued with him the entire time but he acted like I wasn't talking. He just winked at me and kept placing his order and giving the salesman directions.

By the time we got back from eating dinner, which he also was determined to make sure I ate, the furniture was already being delivered. Bethy was standing at the door smiling when we drove up. She was loving this.

"Thank you for letting me do that today. I needed it. You may not understand, but I did," Rush said before I opened the car door.

I glanced back at him. "You needed to buy me an entire bedroom suite and expensive bedding?" I asked confused.

"Yeah, I did."

I didn't understand but I nodded. If he needed to do it then I was going to appreciate it. I still couldn't believe it was all mine. I was going to feel like a princess in my room. "Well, thank you for all of it. I wasn't expecting anything more than a mattress. I wasn't prepared to be spoiled."

Rush leaned forward and pressed a kiss beside my ear. "That's not even close to spoiling you. But I intend to show you exactly what spoiling is."

I shivered and squeezed the door handle. I wasn't going to let him buy me anything else. I had to stop this but the kisses around my ear made it hard to focus.

"Let's go see how it looks," he said as he leaned back.

Space. Had to get some space. I was ready to jump on him right now. Not a good thing. Control. The pregnancy hormones wanted to take over.

Rush was running around the front of the Rover when I opened my door and started to get out. He was in front of me taking my hands and helping me down like I was helpless before I could make a move to get down on my own.

"I can get out myself you know," I told him.

He smirked, "Yeah but where's the fun in that?"

Laughing I pushed past him and made my way toward Bethy who was watching us like we were one of her favorite television dramas.

"Looks like the Pottery Barn decided to unload their latest shipment in your bedroom," Bethy said grinning like a kid in a candy store. "Can I sleep with you in that big ass bed tonight? The mattress is unbelievable!"

"No. She needs her rest. No bed buddies," Rush said walking up behind me and wrapping a protective arm around my waist.

Bethy's eyes dropped to my waist and then back up at Rush. "You know," she said looking very pleased.

"Yes I do," he replied. He tensed up behind me.

I felt horrible. One more person that I had told about my pregnancy before I told him. He had every right to be hurt.

"Good," Bethy said and stepped out of the way so we could walk inside.

"Why don't you go make sure they're putting everything where you want it," Rush said to me when we got inside.

"Good idea." I left him there to go check on the furniture. If he was mad at me he would have time to cool off.

The delivery guys were doing a good job, so I didn't bother them. I was happy with where they were putting things. Walking back to the living room I heard Bethy whispering and I stopped.

"She's better. She's been sick a good bit but the past two mornings she's hasn't thrown up."

"You call me the second she even looks like she might get sick," Rush even managed to make his whisper sound like a demand.

“Yeah, I’ll call you. I wasn’t for the whole don’t tell Rush idea. You did this to her. You need to be there for her.”

“I’m not going anywhere,” he replied.

“You better not.”

Rush chuckled, “If she won’t live with me then at least she has you protecting her.”

“Damn straight. Don’t think I won’t help her disappear if you fuck this up again. You hurt her and she’ll leave.”

“I’ll never hurt her again.”

My chest ached. I wanted to believe him. I wanted to trust him. This was our baby. There was so much that was hard to forgive but I needed to learn how. I did love Rush. I was sure I always would.

I walked into the room and smiled, “They’re putting things right where I want them.”

Rush reached over and pulled me into his arms. He didn’t say anything. He just held me. Bethy left the room and I wrapped my arms around him. It was the first time I didn’t feel alone in a very long time.

Rush hadn’t asked to stay the night. I was kind of surprised. He hadn’t even done anything other than kiss me before he left. That hadn’t done much to cool off my dreams. I woke up once again right before an orgasm. Very frustrated, I threw back my covers and sat up. I had lunch shift again today.

I’d called Woods last night and apologized about running out on him but he understood and asked me if things were okay.

Rush had stood there listening to everything I said so I'd been in a hurry to get off the phone. I would get Woods alone today and talk to him. He was being very understanding.

He did have me in the dining room the rest of the week. The only day he had me on the course was Saturday because it was a tournament. Everyone would be expected to work outside.

When I finally made my way to the kitchen I was greeted with a box of donuts. A small note was attached to the top. Smiling, I picked it up and read.

"*Missed you last night. I couldn't eat these alone. Hope things are better. Love, Jimmy.*"

Crap! I'd forgotten about the donut date. Another person I needed to apologize to. But first I wanted some milk and donuts.

RUSH

I sat down in one of the leather chairs across from Woods desk. He was studying me and it pissed me off. I had been the one to call him and set up this meeting. Why was he so damn amused?

"I'm going to pay you the correct lease amount in full for the condo. I know what the going rate is and I've cut you a check for a six-month lease. Although, Blaire probably won't be living there in six months." I slid the check across his desk.

Woods looked down at it and back up at me. "I assume this is because you don't want me taking care of what is yours."

"That's right."

Woods nodded and picked the check up. "Good. I shouldn't have to take care of Blaire or your baby. But I would have. You may not believe me but I'm glad you know about the pregnancy. Just don't fuck things up. You're gonna have to make sure Nan keeps her claws in."

I didn't need Woods telling me what I did and didn't need to do. None of this was his business. I wasn't done with him just yet so I pissing him off was a bad idea.

"I don't want Blaire working double shifts or outside in the heat. She refuses to stop working but her hours need to be cut back."

Woods crossed his arms over his chest and leaned back in his seat. "She know about this? Because last time I checked she needed all the hours she could get."

"Last time you checked I didn't know she was carrying my baby. Nothing can happen to her, Woods. I can't let anything else happen to her."

He nodded and let out a heavy sigh. "Fine. I agree. I don't like being told what to do but I agree.

"One more thing," I said before standing up. "Jimmy is gay, right?"

Woods burst into laughter then nodded. "Yes, he is but if you could keep that to yourself. The women like to come in just to look at him. He gets tipped well because of it."

Good. I thought he was, but his attachment to Blaire bothered me. "Then I guess he can hover over my girl."

Woods smirked, "I don't think you could stop him if you tried."

My phone rang as I walked to my Range Rover. Pulling my phone out my mother's name appeared on the screen. I'd ignored her for four weeks. I had Blaire back, but I wasn't ready to talk to my mom just yet. I pressed ignore and stuck my phone back in my pocket.

Once I was at Blaire's I checked under the mat and I was happy to see there was no key hidden. I'd talked to her and Bethy last night about how unsafe that was. I knocked on the door and listened to the footsteps on the other side of the door. Bethy's car had been at the club when I left so I knew Blaire was alone. Just thinking about having some time alone with her made me smile.

The door opened and a 'just crawled out of bed' Blaire stood on the other side holding a donut. The blush on her cheeks was adorable. The tiny little tank top barely covering up those big beautiful tits of hers and the little boxer shorts took the adorable and turned her into smoking hot.

I walked inside and closed the door behind me. "Dayum baby," I whispered as I backed her into the sofa. "Please don't ever answer the door looking like this again."

She looked down and then a smile tugged on her lips. "They keep getting bigger. I think it's because of the pregnancy," she said in way of explanation. "I forget they look like this."

I wrapped a lock of her hair around my finger. "Not just the tiny tank top but this sexy just got out of bed hair and—" I slid my hand down over her barely covered up ass "—this needs more covering up too."

"People don't normally stop by in the mornings," Blaire sounded out of breath. I liked knowing I was getting to her.

"Good," I replied. "How did you sleep?" I asked before taking a nip at her earlobe.

"Uh . . . I uh . . . sleep good," she sounded nervous. I pulled back and looked down at her. Why did she sound nervous?

"Only good?" I asked watching as her cheeks turned bright red.

Blaire shifted her feet and looked down at the floor. "Pregnant dreams can be um . . . intense."

"Pregnant dreams? What do you mean?" I was curious now. The fact her entire face was a bright red and she looked ready to crawl under the table and hide from me only made me want to know more.

She started to move and I grabbed her hips and kept her pinned between be and the sofa. "Oh, no you don't. You can't tell me things like that and not explain."

Blaire let out a short unsure laugh and shook her head. "You can keep me here all day but I'm not telling you."

I slipped my hands under her shirt and started to tickle her ribcage. I tried real hard not to focus on the perfectly plump tits just within my reach. I didn't want Blaire to think I only cared about sex with her. So far I'd made our relationship about sex. I wanted to prove to her it was more than that. Even if I was taking cold showers and jerking off thinking about how sweet she'd tasted the other day.

Blaire giggled and squirmed as I tickled her. "Stop!" she squealed and pushed against me. When she tried to squirm away from me my hand slid up and grazed her left breast causing her to freeze. A small sound came from her throat that sounded really close to a moan. I brushed the pad of my thumb over her nipple and she pressed against me. Fuck the no sex thing. How was I supposed to ignore this.

"Please, Rush. I need you," she begged.

She needed me? Wait . . . were her dreams . . . "Blaire, baby, are your dreams about sex?"

She whimpered and nodded as I pinched her nipple between my fingers. "Yes, and I'm tired of waking up horny," she whispered.

Fuck. I took the donut from her hands and laid it down on the table then sucked the glaze from her fingers. Her breathing hitched. I grabbed her and picked her up. She wrapped her legs around my waist and I devoured her mouth while I walked us back to her room. This time there was a big bed for me to put her on and I'd keep her in it all day making love to her if that was what she needed.

I laid her down on the bed and pulled her little shorts and panties off before crawling on top of her. "Get this top off," I said as I yanked it up and over her head. I stopped and looked down at her. Just last week I'd thought I would never see her like this again. Holding her was something I went to bed dreaming about. And now she was here and I wanted to cherish every small portion of her body.

"Rush, please. I need you in me," she squirmed and pleaded. As much as I wanted to worship her body it looked like I wasn't going to get to. I wasn't going to be able to turn down a needy Blaire.

"Can I taste you first?" I asked kissing her mouth again then running kisses down her body.

"Yes, anything. I just need you to touch me," she sighed as my hand found her wet folds and I slipped a finger inside. "Oh, God! Yes, Ahhhh," she cried out as I began touching her.

Sex crazed Blaire was going to be fun. It was like I'd just won the fucking jackpot. I pushed her thighs further apart and lowered my mouth to kiss the hardened little clit hiding there. She bucked and began begging again. Sticking my tongue out I ran it over her swollen sweet spot and both her hands grabbed my hair and held me. I couldn't help but smile.

"Please, Rush, please. You make it feel so good. Please," her sexy little pleadings were about to make me explode. I wanted in her just as bad as she wanted me in there but I was also enjoying this. I focused on making her come in my mouth while she twisted and moaned on the bed. When she finally screamed my name and that she was coming I jumped up and stripped my clothes off in record time.

We didn't need a condom anymore. I came over her and with one easy stroke I was in her. Blaire grabbed onto my shoulders and threw her head back. If this was how all pregnant women were then why the fuck didn't men keep their women knocked up. This was hot. So hot I might not make it very long.

"Fuck me, Rush. Real hard," Blaire panted.

"Baby you keep saying stuff like that and I'm gonna blow before you want me to."

She smiled wickedly up at me. "I'll get you hard again. I promise. Now please do it hard. In my dreams you bend me over and fuck me until I'm screaming and clawing at the bed begging you to never stop. Right before I come, I wake up."

She'd not only been having sex dreams about me but dirty sex dreams about me. I pulled out of her and flipped her on her stomach then jerked her hips up in the air. "You want fucked, sweet Blair. I'll make my girl feel better," I cooed as I ran my hands over her bare ass gently. She started to squirm and I slapped her pussy causing her to gasp in surprise. "If you want it hard, baby, then I'm going to give it to you hard." I promised.

Grabbing her hips I pounded into her and almost shot my load then. She was so fucking tight. The desperate cries of pleasure coming from Blaire weren't helping. Remembering that I needed to make Blaire come again was hard when my balls were drawn up tight and my cock was throbbing.

"Harder," Blaire moaned and I lost it. I began pumping into her with the wild needy abandon that had consumed her. When her tight warmth began squeezing me and my name came tearing out of her mouth I closed my eyes and let go.

BLAIRE

Rush was on his back pulling me to him when I came to from an orgasm I was pretty sure had caused me to black out. I curled up in his arms and sighed in relief. He'd made all the achy needy parts of me very happy. More than happy. I was sore all over and I loved it.

"I think you may have broken me," he chuckled against my temple and placed a kiss there.

"I hope not because when I have energy to move I'd like to do that again," I replied as sweetly as I could.

"Why am I suddenly feeling used," he asked.

I pinched at the skin that covered his abs. "I'm sorry you feel used but with a body like yours what do you expect?"

Rush laughed and rolled me onto my back before covering me with his body. His silver eyes sparkled as he stared down at me. "Is that so?"

I only nodded. I was afraid I'd say something else if I spoke. Like the fact I was in love with him.

"You're so beautiful," he whispered as he lowered his head to kiss my face as if it were something to be cherished.

I wasn't the beautiful one. He was, but I didn't point that out. If he wanted to think I was then I'd let him. His hands ran down my body making it hum with pleasure. "Are you waking up every morning like this?" he asked with a gleam in his eyes.

I could lie, but I'd done enough of that. "Yes. Sometimes in the middle of the night too."

Rush raised an eyebrow, "The middle of the night?"

I nodded.

He reached up and brushed hair out of my face. "How am I supposed to help you in the middle of the night if you're not with me?" his voice sounded truly concerned.

"You don't want me waking you up for sex every night," I told him.

"Baby, if you wake up horny I want to be ready and available," his voice dropped and he slipped a hand down to cup me between my legs. "This is mine and I take care of what's mine."

"Rush," I warned.

"Yes?"

"I'm going to straddle you right here and screw your brains out if you don't stop saying things like that."

Rush grinned. "That isn't much of a threat, sweet Blaire."

I turned my head to grin when the clock on my bedside table

caught my attention. Oh crap! I pushed at Rush. "I have to be at work in ten minutes," I yelled in way of explanation.

Rush moved off me and I jumped out of bed only to realize I was very naked and Rush was lying on the bed watching me panic with a smile.

"Please don't mind me. The view is great from here," he said with a sexy grin.

I shook my head and grabbed a clean pair of panties and a bra then ran to the bathroom.

"Looks like someone got lucky or is that happy smile from all those donuts I brought over?" Jimmy drawled when I walked into the kitchen one minute late.

My face felt like it was on fire. "I loved the donuts. Thank you and I'm sorry I forgot last night. It was a uh . . . crazy day," I replied picking out an apron afraid to make eye contact with him.

"Baby, if I'd just crawled out of bed with Rush Finlay I'd be grinning like mad too. In fact I'm envious as hell. I know my donuts didn't put that satisfied gleam in your eyes."

I started giggling and grabbed a pen and pad. "He is pretty amazing."

"Oh please give me details. I'll hang on every word," Jimmy begged walking out into the dining room beside me.

"Go flirt with women and stop fantasizing about my . . . my," what was Rush? He wasn't my boyfriend. He was my baby daddy and that just sounded cheap.

"He's your man. Say it because it's true. The boy worships at your altar."

I didn't respond. I wasn't sure how to respond. There were tables already filling up and I had a job to do. Woods, Jace, and Thad, the blond with curly hair whose name I hadn't known until recently, were sitting at one of my tables. I went to get the drink orders from Mister Lovelady and his companion today. He always had girls with him that looked like they could be his granddaughters but they never were. According to Jimmy, Mister Lovelady was richer than God. Still he was old. That was just gross.

After I got their drink orders I headed for Woods' table. All three guys smiled at me as I approached and Thad winked. He was a pretty boy who liked to flirt and everyone knew it. So ignoring him was easy. "Good afternoon boys. What can I get you three to drink?" I asked as I sat their water glasses in front of them.

"You look chipper this morning. It's nice to see you smiling again," Thad said as he reached for his glass of water and took a sip.

The blush was back in my cheeks. I could feel it. I glanced over at Woods who was watching me with a knowing look. He was smart enough to figure it out. "I'll have coffee," was Woods only reply. I was extremely thankful he wasn't in the mood to tease me.

"Bethy wouldn't let me touch the donuts Jimmy brought over this morning. I didn't realize donuts would put you in such a good mood," the smirk on Jace's face said he knew exactly what had happened. Was the entire club going to know about my sex life now? Was it that interesting?

"I happen to love donuts," I replied studying my pad instead of looking at any of them.

"I just bet you do," Jace chuckled. "Bring me a Honey Brown, please."

"I feel like I'm missing something here and I hate being left out," Thad said leaning on the table and inspecting me closer.

"Back off and order your damn drink," Woods snapped at him.

Thad rolled his eyes and leaned back in his seat. "Everyone's so touchy. I'll have a bottle of spring water."

I wrote it down then glanced down at Woods. "Would you like me to bring fresh fruit to the table?"

He nodded, "please."

Glad to be done with those three I headed back to the kitchen.

Jimmy was loading up his tray when I walked back into the kitchen. He glanced back at me over his shoulder. "I know I'm being nosy but I gotta ask, who was the girl Rush ran off and left here yesterday?"

Meg. I didn't know anything else about her. Just Meg and old friend. I had actually forgotten that Rush had left her here. "She's an old friend of his. I don't know much else."

"Woods knew her too. He went and talked to her after the

two of you ran off. I figured she wasn't new if they both knew her."

I reminded myself that she was a part of Rush's past. I had no reason to feel jealous of her in any way. They were old friends. Just because she was one of them didn't mean I had to feel inferior.

I put the fruit on my tray and grabbed the drinks everyone had ordered before heading back into the dining room.

I focused on delivering drinks to my tables before doing a sweep of the room while I walked toward Woods' table. I saw Woods cut his eyes from me to a table to my left. It was in Jimmy's area. I glanced back to see if that was a hint for me to help someone when my eyes locked with Rush's. I stopped. He was here. A smile started to form on my lips when my eyes shifted to see Nan sitting beside him with an angry snarl on her face. I swung my attention back to Woods and decided to pretend they weren't here.

"Here's your fruit," I could hear the nervous tone in my voice and I prayed the guys didn't notice. "And here are your drinks. Y'all ready to order now?" I asked forcing a smile.

All three of them stared up at me making this all the more uncomfortable. This was something I was going to have to learn to get over. Nan was his sister. She'd be in my life if Rush was. Learning to live with someone hating me was a part of life I'd need to learn to accept.

"It's his sister. You do this thing with him and you have to deal with her too," Jace told me as if I didn't already know this.

I didn't like feeling like every emotion I had was on display. I'd always been a private person. This was too much.

I ignored him and pulled my pad out and looked pointedly at Woods. He cleared his throat and ordered. The other two did too without anymore words of wisdom.

RUSH

"I called and asked you to have lunch with me. Could you at least give me thirty minutes of your attention? It's been weeks since we've had time alone together. I miss you," the hurt in Nan's voice tugged at me. She was right. I was ignoring her. I wasn't sure what she'd even said since Blaire had walked into the dining room. I'd been so focused on making sure she wasn't carrying anything too heavy and that no one was mistreating her—or flirting with her—that I hadn't been much of a lunch date for my sister.

"Yeah, I'm sorry," I told her and tore my eyes off the door where I'd been waiting on Blaire to walk back through. "Tell me again about this sailing tournament you're doing with the new guy. You said his name was Charles?"

Nan smiled at the mention of the guy's name and then nodded. She reminded me of the little girl I'd hovered over when she looked all excited about something. Not the angry adult she'd grown up to be. "Yes. Charles is the Kellar's grandson. He's from Cape Cod and is big into sailing. He sailed down here for the summer. Anyway there is a sailing tournament he entered and he wants to take me with him. It's just for a few days."

I listened as she rattled on about Charles and his sailboat and tried extremely hard not to look around for Blaire. I needed to find a balance between the two women in my life. Blaire came first, but I loved my sister and she needed me. Even if it was a lunch date listening to her ramble on about her latest conquest. No one else ever listened to her talk.

She stopped talked and scowled at something over my shoulder. "She needs to focus on her work and stop looking over here at you. God, I don't know why Woods doesn't just fire her."

I glanced back to see Woods, Jace and Thad all smiling and joking around with Blaire who was blushing.

"She's not looking now. She's too busy flirting with other guys. She just cares about the money. It's pathetic really. I wish you'd see through her ridiculous act. I mean I can see it—"

"Nan, shut up," I growled and stood up. I hadn't meant to snap, but hearing Nan bad mouth Blaire and watching guys flirt with her and make her blush was a little more than I could handle. I was going to go make sure each one of those horny bastards understood she was mine.

"You're going to leave me for her? She's flirting with them, Rush. I can't believe you would just get up during our lunch to go stake your claim on some cheap whore."

The rage I had been feeling immediately switched its focus

from the guys to my sister. A red haze settled over me as I swung my attention back to her. "What the fuck did you just say?" I asked keeping my voice low and even as I towered over her.

She opened her mouth to speak, but I knew I'd lose it if she said anything else bad about Blaire.

"Don't. If you want to walk out of here with your dignity then don't. If you ever say anything like that about Blaire again I will cut you loose. Do. You. *Fucking*. Understand."

Nan's eyes went wide. I'd never spoken to her this hard before. But she'd gone too far. She jumped up and threw her napkin down on the table. "I can't believe you. I'm your sister. She's just . . . she's just."

"She's just the woman I'm in love with. You need to remember that," I finished for her.

Nan's eyes flashed fire as she spun around and stalked out of the clubhouse. I didn't care. I needed her to leave before I said anything else. I didn't want to hurt her. I loved her but I hated the words that continued to pour out of her mouth.

A hand touched my arm and I jerked in response before I realized it was Blaire. Her blue eyes were full of concern. This was what she'd been afraid of. Nan and her hate. I couldn't blame her but I also couldn't live without her. However, right now I needed to be alone.

"I'm sorry," I whispered then pulled away from her grasp and threw money down on the table before following Nan out of the dining room.

* * *

I spent the next three hours in the gym. My body was physically beat by the time I walked out of there. My anger had faded. I just wanted to see Blaire now. Her shift would be over and I wanted to hold her. She deserved an apology. I should have never taken Nan to the clubhouse to eat. She'd asked that I meet her there for lunch so I'd gone. I'd even made sure we sat in Jimmy's section. I hadn't wanted it to be awkward for Blaire. But it had backfired anyway. That was the last time I allowed Nan near her. If she couldn't get over it, Blaire didn't deserve her anger.

I knocked on the condo door and waited. No one came. I reached into my pocket and pulled out my phone only to be reminded Blaire had no phone. Dammit. I was going to get her phone from my house and force her to take it back. What if she was hurt? What if she'd gone off somewhere and wasn't coming back?

"She's out with Jimmy," Bethy's voice called from behind me. I turned around to see Bethy walking up from the direction of the golf course. "She stopped by after her shift and told me she and Jimmy had a hot date."

"When will she be home?" I asked as Bethy stepped in front of me and unlocked the door.

"Don't know. She was upset. You know anything about that?" Bethy asked in a sour voice as she pushed the door open.

I didn't ask to come in I just followed her in. "Nan and I had lunch at the clubhouse today. It didn't go so well."

Bethy scrunched her nose in disgust. "You think? I can't imagine your bitch of a sister doing anything to upset Blaire." Bethy threw her purse down and muttered a curse word. "She doesn't need the stress you know. She's pregnant and determined to work on her feet and carry trays around all day. You adding your family drama is not what she needs. Next time you want to have family bonding time with the wicked witch could you take it elsewhere?"

She was right. I shouldn't have let Blaire see Nan. I should have never trusted Nan to be nice. Or in the least be civil. This was my fault and I needed to find Blaire.

"Where is she?" I asked

Bethy plopped down on the sofa. "Getting a break from this shit life she's been handed."

If Bethy wanted to hurt me she was doing a damn good job. I was ready to beg when the door opened.

"Sorry I'm late. We went to . . ." Blaire trailed off when her eyes met mine. "Hey."

"Hey," I replied walking over to stand in front of her but afraid to touch her. "I'm so sorry. Please come back to your room and let me explain."

She made the first move and wrapped her arms around my waist. "It's okay. I'm not upset."

She was going to comfort me. Again. That's what she always did was worry about other people. "No it's not," I replied and took her hand to pull her back to her room. Away from Bethy who wasn't my biggest fan right now.

"Go let him grovel. He needs to. Fuck. I need him to," Bethy said from the couch waving us off and grabbing the remote for the television.

BLAIRE

Rush continued to pull me into my room until the door was closed behind us and he was sitting on my bed with me in his lap. I had been upset earlier but I was fine now. He had been in an awful situation and Nan had been upset. I was glad there hadn't been a big scene with me involved for Woods' sake.

"Rush, I promise you that everything is fine. I'm okay," I assured him cupping his face in my hands. Dealing with Nan and her hatred was part of the deal. I got that and I was going to have to live with it if I wanted Rush in my life.

He shook his head. "Nothing about today was okay. I should have never agreed to have lunch with Nan there. I knew better. I should have never trusted her to be a normal person. I'm so sorry, baby. I swear to you that will never happen again."

I covered his mouth with mine and pushed him back on my

bed. "I told you it's okay. Stop apologizing," I whispered against his lips.

Rush's hands slid up my shirt and found my bra that was two sizes too small now. The strap was cutting into my skin after having to wear it all day. He unsnapped it then ran his hands over the skin that was marked from the pressure of the ill-fitting bra.

"You need a new bra," he said brushing his fingers back and forth over my back making me shiver from pleasure.

"Mmmm if you promise to do that every night I'll be fine," I assured him leaning down to kiss him again.

He pulled back, "Why didn't you tell me?" he asked with a pained voice.

Tell him what? I put my hands on either side of his head and lifted myself up to hoover over him. "What is it I was supposed to tell you?" I asked confused.

Rush slipped his hands around my sides until they were sliding under my breasts and I forgot that we were having a conversation. That felt so good. Moaning I pushed my chest into his hands and was getting ready to beg.

"Your skin is cut from this fucking bra, Blaire. Why did you wear it? I'd have gotten you a new one. I'm getting you a new one before you go anywhere else."

He was still talking about my bra. "Rush, I need you to touch me now. Don't worry about my bra. Just please," I bent my head down and took small nips at his shoulder and kissed my way down his chest.

"As good as that feels you can't distract me. I want to know why you didn't tell me your damn bra was hurting you. I don't want you hurting."

I lifted my head and studied him. He was frowning. This really bothered him. No one ever worried about me like this. I wasn't used to it. My heart swelled and I reached down and pulled my shirt and bra off. "Rush. I need a new bra. This one has gotten too small. Would you take me to get one? Please?" I teased as his hands came up and cupped my swollen breasts making me cream in my panties even more.

"Tits as fucking perfect as these need to be taken care of. I can't stand the thought of them being in pain," he smirked up at me, "unless of course I'm the one causing the pain." He pinched both of my nipples hard and I cried out.

"These titties are mine, Blaire. I take care of what is mine," he whispered before pulling a nipple into his mouth.

I just nodded and rocked against him. His erection was pressing against my swollen clit and if I rubbed just a little bit longer I was going to come. I really needed to come.

"Easy girl. Let me get these shorts off you first," he said kissing down to my stomach were he lingered and kissed it sweetly. His eyes lifted to look at me as he slowly unfastened my shorts and began pulling them down my body. "Looks like someone needs some attention. She's all swollen and wet. Dripping wet. Fuck that's hot," he murmured as he pushed my legs apart and gazed hungrily between my legs.

He laid down between my legs until his mouth was so close

to my clit I could feel his warm breath on it. "Tonight I'm staying here. I can't sleep at night knowing you may wake up like this and need me. The idea drives me crazy," his voice dropped to a husky sound that always excited me. I watched as he stuck out his tongue and the silver barbell flashed at me before he ran his tongue through the folds and then slipped it inside me.

I grabbed his head and began pleading with him for more as he brought me to not one but two orgasms before he lifted his head and smiled wickedly at me.

"That's fucking addictive. No one should taste that sweet, Blaire. Not even you."

He stood up and jerked off his shirt then his pants and was back on top of me before I could admire the view for very long.

"I want you to ride me," he said kissing me again while his erection slipped between my legs and teased me.

I pushed him back and he easily rolled over for me so I could climb on top. Watching him as he slowly took in my body was more of a turn on than his naughty words he always whispered in my ears to make me come.

I could love this man and be happy with him the rest of my life. I just hoped I got the chance.

The next few days went by like a fairy tale. I went to work. Rush showed up and distracted me with his gorgeous presence; we ended up having wild sex somewhere we shouldn't before actually going back to my condo or his house and making love in a bed. The second time was always sweet. The first time was always intense and needy on both our parts. I was pretty sure Woods had overheard us the day we'd ended up in the rental closet tearing at each other's clothes.

I was still trying to decide if this was the pregnancy hormones or if I was always going to want Rush like this. One touch from him and I was desperate. Today however we would be on a break. I was working all day at the annual golf tournament. I'd had to fight both Woods and Rush to let me work today. Neither of them had thought it was safe. I, of course, won.

Our cart girl outfits were special ordered for today. We were wearing all white like the golfers and short skirts with polos instead of shorts. Except of course for Jimmy. He'd be in shorts. He was the only male on the drink carts today.

"There are fifteen teams. Blaire you get the first three teams. Then Bethy you have the next three. Carmen you get the next three. Natalie you get the next three and Jimmy you get the last three, they're all women who have requested you specifically. This will be an all day event. Keep the golfers happy and don't run low on drinks. Come back here to restock before you run out of something. Your carts have been pre-stocked with the choice of drink for the golfers you will be trailing today. You each have a walkie talkie in your cart to contact me in case of any emergency. Does anyone have any questions?" Darla stood on the porch of the course offices with her hands on her hips staring down at the five of us.

"Good. Now get to your places. Blaire will be busy right off the bat. The rest of you need to wait on and check on your teams while they're waiting to tee off. If they want a drink get them one. If they want food get them a server. Got it?"

We all nodded. Darla waved us off and went back into the offices.

"I hate tournaments. I just hope I don't have to deal with Nathan Ford. He is so damn annoying," Bethy grumbled as we went to get our carts and make sure we had everything before heading to the first hole.

"Maybe you'll get Jace," I said hoping to cheer her up.

Bethy frowned. "Nope. Not a chance. Aunt Darla did the line up. She won't have given me Jace."

Ah. Well in that case I wouldn't have Rush either. Probably a good thing. I needed to focus on work. Not how good Rush looked in a pair of shorts and a polo.

I parked the cart at the first hole and went to meet my first group. It was familiar faces and they were an older group. They would be easy enough and they were excellent tippers. After getting them all a bottle of water I went to my next group. Surprisingly it was Jace, Thad and Woods. I hadn't expected to have them in my group. "Hello boys. Aren't I the lucky one," I teased.

"I was sure we'd get Bethy. Dayum my day is just now getting better," Thad replied.

"Shut up," Jace grumbled and elbowed him in the side.

"I'm not stupid enough to let Bethy have Jace. She'd ignore everyone else," Woods explained.

I gave all three of them a bottle of water. "I'm happy to serve the three of you. Even if I'm not Bethy," I said smiling at Jace.

"If I can't have Bethy you are definitely my runner-up," Jace said with a crooked grin. I couldn't help but like the guy. He'd more than proved himself with his feelings for Bethy.

"Good. Now, y'all make me proud," I cheered as I headed to the next group. This was my first female group. I recognized them but I wasn't sure exactly who they were. I was pretty sure the tall elegant blond was the mayor's wife.

After I got them their sparkling waters and slices of lime I headed back to the front. It was almost time to start. I glanced back and looked for Rush but didn't see him. I wasn't sure whose team he was on but I knew he was playing. I assumed Grant would be with him but I didn't see him either.

RUSH

I was going to murder Grant in his sleep. Or maybe right here in public with witnesses. I slammed my clubs down and the caddie quickly grabbed them which was a good thing. I was getting ready to throw something.

"Meg? Really Grant? You asked Meg?" I growled looking past Grant to see Meg checking in and pointing our way.

"We needed three. You pissed off Nan so we were short a person. Everyone else was taken. Meg wanted to play. What's the big deal?" Grant handed his bag to the caddie and shot me an annoyed look.

Blaire was the big deal. I hadn't told her that Meg would be on my team because I hadn't known. Now if she saw us she'd think I was trying to keep it from her. I needed to find her.

"Can I get you three a water?" A redheaded cart girl whose name I couldn't remember asked. Figured Woods wouldn't let me have Blaire. That would have helped. I could have explained this to her and she'd been able to see it was completely innocent.

"Yes please, Carmen," Grant replied. He was flashing her a grin and she was batting her eyelashes. He'd probably slept with this one. If not he would tonight. "Give one to grumpy pants too. He needs to hydrate himself," Grant replied.

"Ready to kick some ass?" Meg asked walking up to us.

No I was ready to find Blaire and explain this. I looked back over at the cart girl. "Where in the lineup is Blaire?" I asked her.

She made a pouty face. "I'm not good enough?"

"Yes, sugar, you're perfect. He just has the hots for Blaire. Nothing personal," Grant explained winking at her. She beamed at him again.

"She got the first group. I think Mr. Kerrington is in that group. The young Mr. Kerrington. Mrs. Darla said something about Mr. Kerrington requesting Blaire." The girl replied with a satisfied smile.

Woods was a dick. I didn't doubt it.

"Good morning, Meg. Sorry but we have a bad mood Rush on our hands," Grant said in way of greeting to Meg who I'd forgotten had joined us.

"I can see that. I'm going to go out on a limb here and assume that Blaire is the girl he chased after and left me all alone without an explanation the other day."

"If he chased after a girl then yes it was Blaire," Grant replied.

I ignored both of them and started to walk toward the front

of the line when I saw the first group tee off. Blaire's cart also pulled away at the same time. Shit.

"Would you calm down? Blaire isn't the one to get jealous. That's you," Grant grumbled then took a swig of his water.

"Okay is it a problem that I'm playing with the two of you? Is that what this is about?" Meg asked staring directly at me.

"I don't want Blaire upset," I replied and looked back out in the direction she'd driven off.

"Oh. Well, this is just golf not a date," Meg replied.

She was right. I was being ridiculous. We weren't in high school and I could play golf with a female. Blaire now knew that Meg was an old friend and we were with Grant. It wasn't like it was just the two of us. This would be okay.

"I'm on edge. Sorry. You're right. This isn't a big deal," I agreed and decided to relax and enjoy the day. At least Blaire was in the front. She'd be down and inside sooner. That was probably why Woods had requested her. So she wouldn't be out in the sun as long as the others.

By the time we'd made it to the sixth hole I had relaxed and was enjoying myself. Except for the occasional worry about Blaire being in the heat I was fine. I knew Woods was watching her and as annoying as that was it was also a relief.

"Come on, Grant, so far Rush has the best out of three and I have the best out of two. This one is yours buddy. You can do it," Meg taunted him as he set up to put for par.

Grant shot her a warning glare. Putting wasn't Grant's strong point and it hadn't taken Meg long to figure that out. If he sunk this one it'd be a miracle.

"I think he needs a little help, Meg. Maybe you could go give him a lesson," I suggested.

The angry look on Grant's face made both of us crack up. Damn he was too easy. "You might wanna back up, Meg. He looks ready to blow. If his putter comes flying you don't want to be in the line of fire."

Meg backed up and stood by me. "Does he really throw clubs?" she asked with a hopeful smile.

"Don't get too excited. If he's pissed enough to throw clubs then he is pretty damn mad."

"I'm not scared. You have the bigger arms," Meg said throwing another grin toward Grant. She was goading him.

"He does *not* have bigger arms!" Grant said standing up from his putting stance with a defensive look on his face.

Meg reached over and squeezed my arm. "Um, yeah these are pretty damn impressive. Show me what you got," she teased Grant some more.

Grant jerked his shirt off and walked over to stand in front of Meg flexing his muscles. "Feel that, baby. He aint' got nothing on me. He's just a pretty boy."

Rolling my eyes I started to walk back to the golf cart. Grant reached out and grabbed my arm. "No you don't. This is a contest I'm gonna fucking win. Flex those puny arms. Let her see who is packing more heat."

I had no desire to win this contest. "You won. I'm good with it. He has bigger arms, Meg." I said jerking my arms free of his grip.

"No he doesn't. You weren't flexing when I felt yours and I'm positive yours were bigger," she replied with a wicked grin. I was positive this was a bad idea. I didn't think she was flirting but I wasn't sure.

"That's bullshit! Flex your arm, Rush. I'm proving this one. I got the better guns."

"Yes you do. I'm good with it," I replied.

"Flex them now, I mean it," Grant demanded. He was really in a pissing contest here. One I was gladly willing to let him win. I was just ready to move on to the next hole.

"Fine," I agreed. "If this will make you go putt that ball so we can move on to the next hole I'll flex my arm."

Grant grinned and held his arm out again for her to feel. She was waiting on me. I flexed and let her feel. This was ridiculous.

"Sorry, Grant, he wins this," Meg replied squeezing my arms just a little too long. I dropped my arm and turned and headed back to the cart.

"Putt the ball, Grant," I called out.

"You didn't win this! She just picked you because she feels loyal to you since she was your first fuck," he replied.

I jerked my head around to see if anyone had heard him. Thankfully it looked like no one had.

BLAIRE

I sat there as they got on their cart and drove to the next hole. I was supposed to be getting more drinks, but my desire to see Rush had gotten the best of me and I'd taken a small detour until I found him. Now, I wish I hadn't. For the first time this week I was sick in my stomach again. He hadn't told me Meg was his first. He'd just said they were old friends.

Knowing what kind of old friends they were didn't help. I was well aware that Rush had a string of girls that he'd slept with. It was something I knew when I'd went to his bed the first time. But seeing him with one. The one that had been his first was painful.

She'd been flirting with him and he'd been flirting back. Trying to impress her with his muscles. They were impressive enough without him flexing them and showing off. Why had he done that? Did he want her to be attracted to him? Was he curious about what she was like in bed now?

My stomach rolled and I forced my cart into drive and pulled away from the trees I'd been hiding behind. I hadn't meant to hide. I'd taken a short cut to see if Rush was at this hole. But when I'd seen him smiling at Meg and then letting her touch him I'd stopped. I couldn't go any further.

She fitted into his world. Instead of driving a drink cart around she was playing golf with him. He couldn't have asked me. For starters I had no idea how to play and then of course I worked here. What was he doing with me? His sister hated me. I couldn't be a part of his life. Not really. I would always be on the outside looking in. I hated the way this felt.

Being with Rush was amazing. In the privacy of his house or my condo it was easy to pretend we could be something more. But what would happen when I started showing. When I was very pregnant and he was out with me. How would he handle it? Could I expect him to?

I loaded the cart back up and let my mind play over all the scenarios that could happen with us. None of them ended happily. I wasn't one of the elite. I was just me. This past week I'd let myself play with the idea of staying. Raising this baby with Rush. As much as seeing him with Meg had hurt it had been the wakeup call I needed. No one lived in a fairy tale. Especially me.

By the time I got back my group had made it to the last stretch. I smiled and served drinks and even joked with the golfers. No one was going to know I was upset. This was my job. I was going to be good at it.

Tonight I wouldn't say anything to Rush. There was no point. He wasn't thinking clearly. I would just put some distance between us. I couldn't let myself believe he was my happily ever after. I was smarter than that.

I hadn't been able to make it through the day without getting sick. The heat got to me, but I would be damned if Woods knew about it. I didn't need him thinking I couldn't do my job. Bethy held my hair back while I threw up in the toilet in the back of the offices. I really did love her.

"You over did it," she scolded as I lifted my head up from my last heave.

I didn't want to admit it but she was probably right. I took the wet washcloth she was handing me and cleaned my face before sitting down on the floor and leaning back against the wall.

"I know. But don't tell anyone," I begged.

Bethy sat down beside me. "Why?"

"Because I need this job. The money is good. If I'm leaving once I start showing then I need all the money I can save up. It won't be easy getting a job while I'm obviously pregnant."

Bethy turned her head and looked at me. "You're still planning on leaving? What about Rush?"

I didn't want Bethy mad at him. She just started being nice to him again. "I saw him today. He was having fun. He was where he belongs. I am where I belong. I don't fit in with his world."

"He doesn't get a say in this? If you just said the word he'd have you moved into his house and he would be taking care of everything. You wouldn't be working at this club and you would be at his side everywhere. You've got to know that."

I didn't like the idea of being one more woman who mooched off him. His mother and sister did that. I didn't want to do it too. I didn't care about his money. I just cared about him. "I'm not his responsibility."

"Excuse me if I beg to differ. When he knocked you up you became his ultimate responsibility," Bethy said in a huff.

I knew the truth about the night we'd had sex without a condom. I'd come onto him. I had all but attacked him. It hadn't been his fault. All the other times he was careful. I hadn't let him be that night. It was my mistake not his.

"Trust me when I tell you that this was all on me. You weren't there the night I got pregnant. I was."

"Can't be all your fault. You can't get pregnant alone."

I wasn't going to argue with her. "Just don't tell anyone I was sick. I don't want them worrying."

"Fine. I'm not happy about it though. You do this again and I'm telling," she warned.

I laid my head over on her shoulder. "Deal," I agreed.

Bethy patted my head. "You are one crazy girl."

I just laughed because she was right.

RUSH

As soon as the tournament was over, I went home to shower and clean up. I didn't even hang around to get the second place trophy. I left Grant and Meg to do the honors. I couldn't care less. I only participated in the tournament because I'd signed up with Nan and Grant early in the summer. We did it every year. It was for a good cause.

When I stopped by the offices where the drink carts were parked Darla said Blaire had left with Bethy about an hour ago. I called Bethy but got no answer. I figured by the time I got a shower and changed they would be back from wherever it was they went.

Bethy's car was in the parking lot when I pulled up to their condo. Blaire was home. Thank God. I'd missed her like crazy all day. I knocked three times and waited impatiently for it to open. Bethy gave me a tight smile. Not who I wanted to see.

"Hey," I said stepping in.

"She's already asleep. It was a long day," Bethy said still standing at the door holding it open like she wanted me to leave now.

"Is she okay?" I asked looking down the hall to her closed bedroom door.

"Just tired. Let her sleep," Bethy replied.

I wasn't leaving. She could close the damn door. "I won't wake her up but I'm not leaving. So you can close the door," I told her before heading back to Blaire's room.

It was only six in the evening. She shouldn't be asleep so early unless she was sick. The idea of her overdoing it today made my heart race. I should have insisted she not work today. This wasn't safe for her or the baby.

I opened the door slowly and stepped inside then closed and locked it behind me. Blaire was curled up in the center of her big bed. She looked lost up there. Her long blond hair fanned out over the pillows and one of her long bare legs was kicked out of the covers. I pulled my shirt off then threw it over on the dresser before unzipping my jeans and pulling them off. When I was down to my boxer briefs I pulled the covers back and climbed in behind her and pulled her up against me. She came willingly. A soft sigh and some mumbled greeting was the most adorable sound I'd ever heard. Smiling I buried my face in her hair and closed my eyes.

This was the only place I ever wanted to be. I slid my hand down and laid it flat over her stomach. The idea of what I was holding right now was humbling.

* * *

A soft trail down my arm then across my chest brought a smile to my face as I opened my eyes. Blaire was turned around facing me now. Her eyes were open as she stared at my chest and ran her finger over each of my pecs then back up and across my shoulder. She lifted her eyes and they locked with mine. A small smile played on her lips.

"Hey," I whispered.

"Hey."

It was dark outside now but I had no idea how late it was. "I missed you today."

Her smile slipped and she shifted her gaze away from me. That was an odd reaction. "I missed you too," she replied not looking at me.

I reached up and took her chin so I could turn her gaze back toward me. "What's wrong?"

She forced a smile. "Nothing."

She was lying. Something was definitely wrong. "Blaire, tell me the truth. You look upset. Something is wrong."

She started to pull away from me but I held her close. "Tell me, please." I begged. The tension in her body eased some when I said please. I needed to remember that she was weak where that word was concerned.

"I saw you today. You were having fun . . ." she trailed off.

Was that the problem? Oh . . . wait. She saw Meg. "This is about Meg. I'm sorry, I didn't know until she got there that Grant had asked her to replace Nan. My sister backed out at the last minute and Grant asked Meg to take her spot. I would have told you before if I'd known."

The tension in her body was back. Shit. I thought that explained it. Was she that upset over it?

"She was your first," Blaire's voice was so soft I almost missed it.

Someone had told her. Fuck. Who knew that other than Grant? It wasn't like I shared my sexual history with people. Who could have told her? I cupped her face in my hands, "And you're my last."

Her eyes softened. I was getting good at this sweet talking thing. I hadn't much cared about saying the right thing with females before. It was easy with Blaire. I was just being honest.

"I . . ." she stopped and wiggled in my arms. "I need to go to the restroom," she said. I was positive that wasn't what she was going to say at first but I let her go so she could get up.

She was wearing a yellow tank top and pair of pink panties that I knew girls referred to as boy shorts. Even though no guy I knew would wear something like that. Her hips looked fuller and the idea of bending her over the bed and holding onto those hips made me hard as a rock. I needed to focus. Blaire was upset about something and she wasn't telling me what it was. I had to fix this. I didn't want her upset.

My phone rang and I reached over to get it off the nightstand. It was Nan. Not who I wanted to talk to at the moment. I pressed ignore checked the time and then turned my ringer off. It was only ten after nine.

Blaire stepped back out of the bathroom and grinned sheepishly. "I'm kinda hungry."

"Then let's go get some food," I said getting up and reaching for my jeans.

"I need to go to the grocery store. I was going to go earlier but I was sleepy so I thought I'd take a nap first."

"I'll take you to dinner then we'll go grocery shopping in the morning. There are no grocery stores open this late around here."

Blaire looked confused. "There aren't any restaurants in town open either."

"The club is open until eleven. You know that." I yanked my shirt down over my head then walked over to her. She was studying me like she didn't understand.

"What?" I asked grabbing her waist and pulling her almost naked body up against me.

"People will see you with me at the club. People other than your friends," she said slowly as if letting it sink in.

"And?" I asked.

She tilted her head back so she could look up at me. "And I work there. They know I work there."

I still didn't understand what she was saying. "I'm not following you."

Blaire let out an exasperated sigh. "Do you not care that other club members will see you eating dinner with an employee?"

I froze. What? "Blaire," I said slowly making sure I'd heard her correctly. "Did you just ask me if I cared if someone saw me eating with you? Please tell me I misunderstood that."

She shrugged.

I dropped my hands from her waist and walked over to the door needing to put distance between us. She had to be kidding me. When had I ever led her to believe that I was ashamed of her?

I looked back at her. She had crossed her arms over her chest as she watched me.

"When have I ever made you think I didn't want to be seen with you? Because if I have then I swear to you I'll fix it."

She shrugged again. "I don't know. We've just never really gone out on a date. I mean there was the honky tonk that time but it wasn't really a date. Your social functions normally don't include me."

My chest constricted. She was right. I'd never taken her anywhere other than to buy furniture and given her a ride to Sumit and back. Fuck. I was an idiot. "You're right. I suck. I've never taken you anywhere special," I whispered then shook my head. I had never really had a relationship before. I fucked girls then I sent them home.

"So all this time you thought I was ashamed of you?" I asked knowing I didn't want to hear the answer. It was going to hurt like a motherfucker.

"Not ashamed exactly. I just . . . I just thought, well, I don't fit into your world. I know that. Just because I'm pregnant with our baby doesn't mean you have to claim me in any way. You're just being supportive—"

"Blaire. Please. Stop now. I can't listen to any more." I closed the distance I'd put between us. "You're my world. I want everyone to know. I don't know how to date so I never even thought of taking you on a date. But I can promise you right now. I will be taking you on so many damn dates that there won't be a person in this town that doesn't know I worship the ground you walk on," I swore before reaching out and taking her hand. "Forgive me for being an idiot."

Blaire blinked back tears and nodded. I wondered how many more times I was going to screw up before I ever got this right.

BLAIRE

The cell phone Rush had bought for me was sitting on the kitchen bar when I walked out of my room. This was the third time this week he'd left it somewhere for me to find. This time it had a note attached.

I picked it up. "Think about the baby. You need this for emergencies."

That was a low blow. Smiling I picked the phone up and put it in my pocket. He wasn't going to give up until I accepted it. Today was my second doctor's appointment. I'd told Rush about it on our third date Monday night. He'd been determined to take me on dates all week. Last night I'd begged him to let us just stay in and watch a movie. He had made his point. Everyone in town had seen us together. I was sure they were all sick of seeing us together by now. The thought made me smile even more.

I slipped the phone back out of my pocket. I had forgotten to remind Rush about today's appointment last night. Now I had a phone so I could call him. His name was the first one on my contacts list under favorites. I wasn't surprised.

It rang three times before he answered.

"Hey, I need to call you back," Rush's said in an annoyed tone.

"Okay but," I started to say when he muffled the phone to talk to someone else. What was going on?

"Are you okay?" he snapped.

"Yeah, I'm fine but—"

"Then I gotta call you back." He interrupted me before I could finish then he ended the call.

I sat there and stared at the phone. What had just happened? Maybe I should have asked if he was okay. When he didn't call back in the next ten minutes I decided I'd better get dressed for my appointment. Surely he would call back before it was time to leave.

An hour later and he still hadn't called back. I debated on calling him back or not. Maybe he had forgotten that I called. I could always borrow Bethy's car and go to my appointment. On Monday when I'd told him about it he'd seemed excited about going. I couldn't just leave without him.

I pressed his number again. It rang four times this time.

"What?" Nan's voice startled me. Was he at Nan's?

"Uh, um," I wasn't sure what to say to her. I couldn't tell her about my appointment. "Is Rush there?" I asked nervously.

Nan let out a hard laugh. "Unbelievable. He told you he'd call you back. Why don't you give him some breathing room. Rush doesn't do needy. He's with his family visiting. My mom and dad are here and we're getting ready to go and have a family lunch. When he is ready to talk to you he will." Then she hung up.

I sank down onto the bed. He was having a family lunch with his sister, mother and my father. That was why he hung up on me? He didn't want me to know he was with them. His family lunch came before me and the baby. This was what I expected all along, but then he'd been so sweet and protective. Was I being needy? I wasn't a needy person but I had turned into one. Hadn't I?

Standing up I laid the phone down on the bed. I didn't want it anymore. Nan's hateful voice as she told me they were eating with *her* father taunted me. I grabbed my purse. I had time to walk down to the offices and borrow Bethy's car before my appointment.

I was sweating by the time I made it to the course offices. So much for looking nice for my appointment. That didn't matter really. It was the least of my problems. I walked up the steps and Darla met me as she was coming out of the door.

"You not on to work today," she stated when she saw me.

"I know. I need to borrow Bethy's car. I have a doctor's appointment in Destin that I . . . uh . . . forgot about." I hated lying but telling her the truth was just more than I could handle.

Darla studied me a moment then reached into the pocket of her slacks and pulled out her keys. "Take my car. I'll be here all day. I don't need it."

I wanted to hug her, but I didn't. I wasn't sure she'd be comfortable with that kind of reaction to a simple doctor's appointment. "Thank you so much. I'll put gas in it," I assured her.

She nodded and waved me on. I hurried down the steps and climbed into her Cadillac and headed toward Destin.

The drive over wasn't bad and I only had to wait fifteen minutes before they called me back to the exam room. The nurse was all smiles as she pulled out a machine with a small screen on it.

"You're only nine weeks along so to hear the baby's heartbeat we're gonna need to do an ultrasound. We should hear the heartbeat and see a little bitty baby in there too," she explained.

I was going to hear my baby's heartbeat and see it. This was real. The few times I'd imagined this day I hadn't imaged it alone. I had thought someone would be with me. What if they can't find a heartbeat? What if something is wrong? I didn't want to be alone for this.

The doctor walked in with a comforting smile. "You look terrified. This is a happy moment. All your vitals are good. No need to be so nervous. He assured me. "Now lay back." I did as he instructed and the nurse put my legs up in the stirrups.

"You aren't far enough along to so this externally and see or hear the baby. We need to do a transvaginal ultrasound which means we need to go in vaginally. It doesn't hurt. You'll feel some pressure from the wand. That is all," the nurse explained.

I didn't watch them. The idea of him sticking something up me only made this worse. I focused on the screen.

"Okay here we go. Easy, be still," the doctor instructed. I watched the black and white screen waiting patiently for something that resembled a baby.

A small thumping sound filled the room and it felt like my own heart had stopped beating.

"Is that?" I asked suddenly unable to say anything else.

"That's it alright. Thumping just right too. Nice and strong," the doctor replied.

I stared at the screen and the nurse pointed to what looked like a little pea. "There he or she is. Perfect size for nine weeks."

I couldn't swallow past the lump in my throat. Tears rolled down my face but I didn't care. I just sat transfixed looking at the screen at that tiny little miracle while his heartbeat filled the room.

"You and the baby are both doing really well," the doctor said as he slowly pulled the instrument from inside of me and the nurse pulled down my gown and gave me her hand to pull me up.

"If you experience a little blood-tinged discharge, it's perfectly normal after this procedure. Don't be alarmed," the doctor said standing up and going over to the sink to wash his hands.

"Keep taking those prenatal vitamins and come back and see me in four weeks."

I nodded. I was still in awe.

"Here you go," the nurse said handing me a small pictures from my ultrasound.

“These are mine?” I asked looking down at the picture of my baby.

“Of course they are,” she replied with an amused tone.

“Thank you,” I said as I looked at each one and found the small pea I knew was alive inside me.

“You’re welcome.” She patted my knee. “You can get dressed now. Everything looks great.”

I nodded and wiped away another tear that had broken free and was rolling down my face.

RUSH

"Where is she, Bethy?" I demanded walking out of Blaire's bedroom holding her cell phone. She'd left it here.

Bethy snarled at me and slammed a kitchen cabinet door. "The fact your sorry ass doesn't know where she is only makes me hate you more."

What the fuck was wrong with her? I'd had a day from hell. Telling my mom she had to get another house and then telling them I was going to ask Blaire to marry me had sent them all into a wild rage. Well, not all of them. Blaire's father had seemed fine with it. Nan and my mother had gone ballistic. We'd spent several hours yelling at each other and I'd made threats I intended to keep. Nan was supposed to leave to go back to school on Monday. She'd be gone until winter break and I was sure she'd end up in Vale with friends then. It was what she did every year. Normally I went too but not this year.

"I've had to deal with my mother and sister for the past four hours. Kicking Georgianna out of the house and informing her and Nan that I intend to ask Blaire to marry me wasn't exactly an easy battle. So forgive me if I need a little help remembering where Blaire is!"

Bethy sat the bottle of water down on the bar and her angry snarl became more of a disgusted frown. I'd thought once she heard I was going to propose to Blaire that she'd be happy. Apparently not.

"I hope you didn't buy a ring," was her only response.

I was tired of her games. "Tell me where she is," I roared.

Bethy put both her hands on the bar and leaned forward giving me a furious scowl I didn't know the girl was capable of. "Go. To. Hell."

Fuck. What had I done?

The door opened and Blaire came walking in smiling until her eyes met mine. Then her smile faltered. She was mad at me too. Not good.

"Blaire," I said as I walked toward her and she started backing up.

"Don't," she replied holding up both her hands to stop me from coming closer.

She was holding something. It looked like pictures. What the hell did she have pictures of? Was it something from my past? Was she pissed about some girl I'd done something with once?

"Is that what I think it is?" Bethy asked pushing past me and running to Blaire.

Blaire nodded and handed her the pictures. Bethy covered her mouth, "Oh my God. Did you hear the heartbeat?"

At the words "heartbeat" my chest felt as if it had just been ripped wide open. Understanding dawned on me. Today was Thursday. It was Blaire's doctor's appointment. She'd called to remind me and I'd hung up on her.

"Blaire, shit, baby, I am so sorry. I was dealing with my—"

"Your family. I know. Nan told me when I called back. I don't want to hear your excuses. I just want you to leave," her voice was flat. There was no emotion in it.

She turned her attention back to the pictures and pointed to something. "Right there. Can you believe that's inside me?"

Bethy turned her hateful scowl from me to the picture and a soft smile touched her face. "It's amazing."

They were standing there looking at pictures of my baby. Blaire had heard his heartbeat today. Alone. Without me.

"Can I see?" I asked scared she'd tell me no or worse ignore me.

Instead, she took the pictures from Bethy and handed them to me. "The little thing that looks like a pea. That's . . . our baby," she finished. She had been reluctant to call it our baby. I couldn't blame her.

"Was its heart okay? I mean did it beat properly and everything?" I asked staring down at the picture in my hand.

"Yes. They said everything was perfect," she replied. "If you want it you can keep that one. I have three. But I'd like for you to leave now."

I wasn't leaving. Bethy standing guard wasn't going to stop me either. I would say all this in front of Bethy if I had to but I refused to leave this condo.

"My mother and your father showed up unannounced today. Nan leaves for college Monday. Mom thought I'd be leaving too so she was back to move in for the year. I informed her I wasn't leaving and she'd need to find another home. I also informed them that I was staying until you decided you wanted us to move somewhere else. That I intended to ask you to marry me," I paused and watched as her face paled. Not the reaction I was hoping for. "It didn't go over well. There was a lot of yelling. Hours of screaming and threats. When you called me I had just announced to the three of them that I was going to marry you. All hell had broken loose. I was going to call you back once I had my mother and Abe back in their car and headed out of town. I didn't want you to have to face either of them. But my mother doesn't go down without a fight. Nan packed up and left for school this evening. She is refusing to ever speak to me again," I stopped and took a breath.

"I can never tell you how sorry I am. The fact I forgot about today's appointment is unforgivable. I keep having to apologize to you. I wish I could stop fucking everything up."

"You weren't going to have lunch with your family?" she asked.

"What? No!"

The rigid stance of her posture relaxed. "Oh," she said in a sigh.

"Why did you think I'd go to lunch with them? I wouldn't hang up on you to go spend time with them."

"Nan," she replied with a sad smile.

"Nan? When the hell did you talk to Nan?" I'd been with Nan all morning.

"When I called you back. Nan answered and said you didn't have time for me you were going to eat with your family."

My lying little sister better be glad her ass was headed back to the east coast because I'd go ring her neck if I could get my hands on her.

"You went to that appointment thinking I'd blown you and our baby off for them? Fuck!" I pushed past Bethy and pulled Blaire into my arms. "You are my family, Blaire. You and this baby. Do you understand me? I missed something important today I will never forgive myself for. I wanted to be there and hear the heartbeat. I wanted to be holding your hand when you saw him for the first time."

Blaire tilted her head back and smiled up at me. "You know it could be a girl."

"Yeah, I know."

"Then stop calling our baby a 'him'," she replied.

Smiling I kissed her forehead. "Can we go back to your room and you tell me about the appointment. I want to know everything."

She nodded and glanced over at Bethy. "Are you going to continue scowling at him are or you going to forgive him?"

Bethy shrugged, "Not sure yet."

BLAIRE

School was back in session. Vacationers and summer people had gone home. The club had a lot less traffic and because of this tips were down. The biggest thing was that Rush hadn't mentioned the proposing thing again since the night at the condo when he'd said that was what he'd told his family. I wondered sometimes if he'd changed his mind or I'd imagined it.

If it wasn't for Bethy asking me weekly if Rush had brought it up again I would think it had been a figment of my imagination. Every time I told her no he hadn't she got more and more agitated. Not to mention my heart hurt a little more. I was afraid Rush'd thought it through and decided it was a mistake. Before he'd mentioned it that night I hadn't even let myself believe he'd want to marry me. I figured we'd raise the baby from two different homes. If my thoughts went to the future I would block it out. It wasn't something I wanted to hope for.

My hours at the club were being cut back due to the slower season and I wondered if I needed to get a second job, but there wasn't a lot to choose from around here and it was very likely that Rush wouldn't take it well.

When I stepped into my bedroom there was two things that caught my attention. There were rose petals on my bed and in the center of them was an envelope with my name written neatly across the front. I picked it up and opened it. The stationary was expensive feeling and at the top of it "Finlay" was embossed.

Meet me down at the beach.

Love,

Rush

His abnormally perfect handwriting made me smile. I went to my closet and pulled out a white sundress that had two black stripes across at the hem. If he had planned a romantic something at the beach I wasn't going to wear my work clothes.

After brushing my hair and touching up my makeup I headed out the french doors that faced the gulf and made my way down to the beach. Rush was dressed in a pair of khaki shorts and a button up shirt. I was glad I'd changed. His back was to me and his hands were in his pockets as he stood there staring out at the water. I wanted to stop and admire him but I was also anxious to see him. He'd been gone when I woke up this morning.

I stepped off the walkway and onto the sand. It was oddly deserted except for the two of us. Even though the crowds were down it was still eighty-eight degrees and sunny outside. Glancing down I noticed something in the sand. Someone had written in it. There was a stick lying off to the side.

I stopped and read aloud, "Blaire Wynn, will you marry me?" as the words sunk in Rush walked across the words and knelt down on one knee in front of me.

A small box appeared in his hand and he opened it slowly as a diamond ring caught the fading sun and appeared to come alive as it sparkled. It was happening. Did I want this? Yes. Did I trust him? . . . Yes.

Was he ready? I wasn't sure.

I didn't want this to be something he was doing because he felt pressured to. It would be easy to reach down and take the ring and put it on my finger. But was it what Rush really wanted?

"You don't have to do this," I forced myself to say staring down at him. He hadn't spoken to his sister or his mother in weeks. As much as I disliked them . . . no hated them, I didn't want to be what came between him and his family.

Rush shook his head. "I don't have to do anything. But I *want* to spend the rest of my life with you. No one but you."

His words were the right words. I still felt like something was wrong. He couldn't truly want this. He was young, rich, and gorgeous. I had nothing to offer him. I'd tie him down. Change his world. "I can't do this to you. I can't hinder your future. You can go do anything. I promised you I'd let you be a part of our baby's life. That won't change when you feel like you're ready to leave. I'll always let you"

"Don't say another word. I swear, Blaire, I am seconds away from throwing your ass in that ocean," he stood up and his steady gaze held mine. "No man has ever loved a woman as much as I love you. Nothing will ever come before you. I don't know what else I have to do to prove to you but I won't let you down again. I won't hurt you. You don't have to be alone anymore. I need you."

Maybe this wasn't right and maybe I was making a mistake but his words tugged at corners of my heart he had somehow not managed to reach until that moment. I took the box from his hand and lifted the ring free. "Yes," I said and slipped the ring on my finger.

"Thank God," he whispered then captured my mouth in a hungry kiss. This was real and maybe it wouldn't be forever but it was mine now. I'd find a way to let him go if he wanted to. But I loved him. That would never change.

"Move in with me," he begged.

"I can't. I have to pay my half of the lease," I reminded him.

"I paid your lease in full for a year. Every dime you've given Woods has gone into a savings account with your name on it. So has Bethy's. Now, please move in with me."

I wanted to get mad at him for lying about the money, but right now I couldn't. I pressed another kiss to his lips and then nodded.

"And please stop working," he added.

"No," I replied. I wasn't doing that.

"You're my fiancé now. You're going to be my wife. Why do you want to work at a country club? Don't you want to do something else? What about college? Do you want to do that? Is there a degree you want? I'm not trying to take away your choices, I just want to give you more."

I was going to be his wife. Those words sunk in as I gazed up at him. I didn't have to give up college like I had high school. I could get a degree and have a profession.

"I want that. Just let me soak this in first. Too much, too fast," I said wrapping my arms around him.

RUSH

Blaire was determined to work out a two weeks notice with Woods. I wasn't going to argue with her. She'd agreed to everything I asked. I wasn't about to push my luck. I sat at the table with my laptop and a cup of coffee waiting for her to get off her shift.

Woods had stopped by to talk to me for a few minutes but other than that it had been a quiet evening. Most everyone had left town. Jace was hanging around because of Bethy but I wasn't sure he was going to make it much longer. I'd seen the restless look in his eyes the other day when we'd played a round of golf. He wasn't used to staying in this town longer than a summer.

"This seat taken?" I looked up to see Meg take the seat across from me. I hadn't seen her much since the golf tournament. I glanced back to see Blaire refilling someone's water but her eyes were on me.

“Yeah, it is,” I replied without looking back at Meg.

“I know you’re engaged to the blond. Everyone knows it. I’m not here to hit on you,” she replied.

Blaire smiled at me and then turned to walk back to the kitchen. Shit. What did that smile mean?

“She has a big ass diamond on her hand. She has nothing to be worried about and she knows it. Calm down, dude. You’re freaking out over nothing.”

I shifted my attention to Meg. “She knows you were my first. It bothers her.”

Meg chuckled, “I can assure you the memories I have from our experience and the reality she is living in is two different planets. I got the horny virgin. She has the seasoned pro.”

I glanced back to see if Blaire was back out here. I didn’t want her hearing this. “Just go sit somewhere else. She’s emotional right now. I don’t want her upset.”

No one knew she was pregnant yet. I was letting Blaire decide when to tell people.

“She’s not made of china. She will not break. Does she know you treat her like a damn doll?”

“Yes, I do. We’re working on that,” Blaire replied as she approached out table and poured more coffee into my cup. “I don’t believe we have officially been introduced. I’m Blaire Wynn,”

Meg took a quick startled peek at me then turned back to Blaire. “Meg Carter.”

“It’s nice to finally meet you, Meg. Can I get you something to drink?”

This was not what I'd been expecting. Not that I didn't like it because I did. It meant I was making her feel more secure with me.

"If I ask for a Diet Coke is Rush going to take a swing at me?" Meg asked.

Blaire laughed and shook her head. "No. He'll be a good boy. I promise." Then she looked down at me, "You hungry?"

"I'm good," I assured her.

She nodded and headed back to the kitchen.

"I might just be in love with her a little bit." Meg said. "She's smoking hot and seems smart too. But then if someone is going to tie *you* down then they'd have to be a complete package."

Smiling I took a sip of my coffee. Then looked back at the doorway waiting on Blaire to walk back through. I couldn't wait to get her sexy little ass home.

Blaire kept leaning over the seat pressing kisses down my neck and nibbling my ear. It was real damn hard to stay focused on driving back to the house.

"I'm about ready to pull over and fuck my horny little fiancé if she doesn't stop," I warned taking a nip at her bottom lip when she kissed too close to my mouth.

"That sounds like more of a promise than a threat," she teased slipping her hand between my legs and cupping my erection.

"Fuck, baby, you're driving me crazy," I growled pressing into her hand.

"If I suck it can you concentrate enough to drive?" she asked as she started unbuttoning my jeans.

"I'll more than likely run us into a palm tree but I don't give a shit at the moment," I replied as her hand slipped down the front of my underwear.

Luckily we wouldn't have to find out. I pulled into the driveway and slammed the car in park just as Blaire got my pants unzipped. My phone went off for the third time. I'd had it on vibrate and private so it wouldn't disturb us by flashing up on the screen. My mother had called me earlier while I'd been waiting on Blaire and I wasn't in the mood to answer it. Once it stopped it started back again. Damn. I was going to have to either turn it off or deal with her. Blaire had my cock in her hands so I was thinking that off would work best. Glancing down I noticed an out of area number flashing across my screen. The area code was familiar but I couldn't place it.

"Who is it?" Blaire asked.

"Not sure but they're determined."

Blaire stopped touching me. "Answer it. I'll be good for a few minutes."

I pressed answer. I needed to get rid of them and get my girl inside. But before I could say hello my mother started talking and my world was jerked out from under my feet.

BLAIRE

Rush's face went pale. I grabbed his hand but he didn't react. He sat there listening to the person on the other line without speaking. The more they talked the whiter he got. My heart was racing. Something terrible had happened. I kept waiting for him to say something. Anything. But he didn't.

"I'm on my way," he said in a flat voice before dropping his phone to his lap and moving his hand from my grasp to grip the steering wheel.

"What's wrong, Rush?" I asked more scared now than I had been while he was on the phone.

"Go inside the house, Blaire. I have to go. Nan's been in an accident. Some damn sailboat," He closed his eyes tightly and muttered a curse. "I just need you to get out of the car and go inside. I'll call you when I can but I have to go, now."

"Is she hurt? Can't I go with you?"

"NO!" he roared still looking straight ahead. "You can't go with me. Why would you even ask that? My sister is in ICU and unresponsive. I need to go to her and I need you to get out of the car."

He was hurting and scared. I understood that. But I wanted to be there for him. I loved him and I didn't want him hurting alone. "Rush please let me go with you—"

"GET OUT OF THE CAR!" He yelled so loudly my ears stung. I fumbled for the door handle and grabbed my purse.

He reeved the engine and continued to stare straight ahead while his knuckles turned as white as his face from gripping the steering wheel so tightly. I wanted to say more but he was so upset I was scared of what he would do. He didn't want to hear me speak nor did he want to look at me.

I didn't want to cry in front of him. That wasn't what he needed right now. I got out of the car as quickly as I could. Before I could get the door fully closed he threw the car in reverse and spun out of the drive. I just stood there and watched as he drove away. I couldn't help him. I wasn't wanted.

Tears ran down my face freely now. He was hurting. My heart broke for him. Once he got there and saw her he would call me. I had to believe that. I wanted to call him and make him talk to me but my ears still rang and my heart still hurt from his words.

I finally turned to look back at the house. It was large, sprawling and dark. Nothing was welcoming about it without Rush. I didn't want to stay here alone but I didn't have a car to drive to Bethy's either. I shouldn't have moved from Bethy's. It had been too soon. Everything with Rush had moved so fast. Now, it was all about to be tested. I wasn't sure I was ready for that test. Not yet.

Calling Bethy and telling her I would need a ride to work the next day and that Rush had left wasn't something I was up for tonight. She would find something wrong with this and make me feel even worse. I understood Rush's fear and the way he reacted and left but Bethy wouldn't. At least I didn't think she would. Rush had won some points in his favor when he put the ring on my finger in her eyes and I wanted to keep it that way.

I opened my purse to get out the house keys when I realized I hadn't brought them. Rush had taken me to work, so I hadn't thought I needed them. Looking back up at the dark house I was almost relieved that I wouldn't have to be staying there alone tonight.

The club was only three miles from here. I could walk that. Then Bethy's was just a short walk from the club. The evening breeze had cooled things down and it wasn't so bad. I slipped my purse back over my shoulder and started walking down the brick paved driveway toward the road.

It took about an hour and fifteen minutes to get to Bethy's. Her car wasn't in the parking lot. There was a good chance she was staying with Jace tonight. I guess I should have thought about that. I stopped and looked at the door to the condo. I didn't have the energy to walk back. My stubbornness not to call for a ride was biting me in the butt.

I bent down and lifted the mat. There on the cement slab was the spare key. She must have put it back out after I moved.

She'd only stopped hiding it there because I had asked her to. Tonight it came in extremely handy. I doubted she was coming home until tomorrow anyway. I didn't have to tell her about all this tonight.

I carried the key inside with me and then headed back to my bathroom to take a shower. Rush had insisted Bethy keep the bed he'd bought in the second bedroom instead of taking it when I moved out. Something else I could be thankful for tonight.

I managed to get to work the next day without Bethy ever knowing I'd needed to crash at her place. It wasn't that I thought she'd care but I wasn't ready to answer her questions or hear her opinions.

After changing into a clean uniform from the supply room I made my way to the kitchen. Just before I reached the door Woods stepped out and leveled his gaze on me.

"I was looking for you," he said and nodded his head toward the hallway that led to his office. "We need to talk."

He more than likely knew about Nan. I was sure everyone in their circle did by now. Was he going to ask me about her? I really hoped he wasn't. Admitting that I knew nothing made me sound like I didn't care. Did Rush think I didn't care? Was it my responsibility to call him? He was the one hurting. His reaction last night had scared me but if he needed me I had to get over that.

"Did you sleep at all?" Woods ask looking back at me.

I nodded. I hadn't really slept well but I had gotten some

sleep. The three mile walk had helped exhaust me to the point that I couldn't keep my eyes open once I laid down.

Woods opened his door and held it so I could go inside. I went in and walked over to stand beside the chairs that sat across from his desk. He walked over and stood in front of his desk and sat on the edge of it while crossing his arms over his chest.

A frown wrinkled his forehead as he studied me. I was beginning to wonder if this was about something else. I'd thought it was about Nan, but maybe it wasn't. Had I done something wrong?

"I got a call from Grant this morning. He's at the hospital and he's worried about you. He said Rush showed up in the middle of the night and was in a rage. Seeing as how for the first time in their life Nan and Rush hadn't been on talking terms and now that she is in this condition, Rush isn't taking it well. Grant was concerned as to how he left you and if you were okay."

My heart hurt. I hated to know Rush was in so much pain and there was nothing I could do. He wasn't calling me and that only led me to believe he didn't want to talk to me. I was the reason for his rift with Nan. I was the reason he hadn't spoken to her in weeks. I was the reason he was going through. Tears stung my eyes. As much as I didn't want to admit this, I was the reason this was even harder on Rush. If I hadn't caused their fight then he wouldn't be living with the guilt I knew he was swimming in right now.

This was why Rush and I would never work. Believing in

the fairy tale had been amazing. But it hadn't been real. We'd been biding our time until it came crumbling down. He needed his family right now. I wasn't his family. I wasn't even accepted by his family. How did I fit into this?

"I . . . I don't know what to do?" I choked out hating that Woods was going to see me cry. I didn't want him to see me cry. I didn't want anyone to.

"He loves you," Woods said gently. I wasn't even sure he believed those words. Not now. Maybe Rush had thought he loved me, but how could he when I'd caused him to turn on Nan and now he may lose her.

"Does he?" It was a question I needed to ask myself not Woods.

"Yes. I've never seen Rush with anyone the way he is with you. Right now . . . the next few days or weeks however long this lasts it may not feel like it. But he does. I'm not telling you this because for Rush. He's an ass and I owe him nothing. I'm telling you this for you. It's the truth and I know you need to hear it right now."

I shook my head. I didn't need to hear it. Thinking clearly and deciding what was best for me and my baby was what I needed to do. Could I bring a child into a world that may never accept it?

"I can't tell you what to believe. But if you need anything, I'm here. I know Rush has a garage full of cars, but if you don't want to drive one then I can give you a ride to the doctor or the store. Just call me if you need me."

My next doctor's appointment was in five days. How was I going to get into the house? And he'd never shown me where the keys to his cars were or given me permission to drive them.

"I'm locked out of the house. He thought I had my key when he left," I told Woods.

"Where did you stay last night?" he asked dropping his hands from his chest and standing up. He looked angry. I hadn't meant to make him mad. I was just stating a problem I had. All my clothes were in Rush's house.

"Bethy's."

"How did you get there?"

"I walked."

"Shit! Blaire that is three and a half miles at least. It was dark last night when Rush left. You have a phone now, use it." He was yelling.

"I wanted to walk. I needed to walk. Don't yell at me," I raised my voice and glared at him.

The tension in Woods' shoulders left and he sighed. "I'm sorry. I shouldn't have talked to you like that. It's just that you're so damn determined to be independent. Let me make myself clear. Call me if you ever need a ride. I like to think we're friends. I help my friends."

I needed friends. "I like to think we're friends too," I replied.

He nodded, "Good. But as your boss I'm not letting you work today. I'll have you in Rush's house within the hour. I'll drive you there myself."

Before I could ask him how he had his phone to his ear.

"I've got her in my office. She's locked out of the house." He paused. "No shit. She walked to Bethy's last night. I'm going to take her there if you can get Rush's housecleaner to go unlock the place." He paused again. "No problem. Happy to help. Keep me updated, I'm thinking about y'all." He hung up and looked at me. "Grant's having the housecleaner open the house. You go get something to eat from the kitchen here and then we can head that way. He said to give her about twenty minutes."

I wasn't hungry but I nodded. "Okay," I started for the door then stopped and turned to look back at him. "Thank you."

Woods winked. "My pleasure."

RUSH

I sat in the leather chair beside the hospital bed and stared at my little sister. She hadn't opened her eyes. The monitors blinked and beeped telling me she was alive. Her still form on the bed with gauze wrapped around her head and needles in her arms made it feel as if she were gone. The last words I'd said to her had been hard. They seemed cruel now. I'd just wanted her to grow up. Now that might never happen.

The rage I'd felt when I arrived had been knocked out of me when I laid eyes on Nan. Just seeing her so broken and helpless was killing me. I just needed her to open her eyes. I needed to tell her I loved her and I was sorry. I'd promised her that she'd always have me. No matter what. Then I'd jerked that away from her. Because she couldn't accept Blaire.

My stomach knotted up thinking of how I'd left Blaire. Her eyes had been wide and terrified. I'd handled leaving her all wrong, but I'd been terrified myself. I couldn't call her yet. Not while Nan was like this. I'd already put Blaire before Nan and look where that got me. This time Nan needed to come first. If she knew I was sitting here waiting on her she'd open her eyes. I knew she would.

The door opened and Grant stepped in. His eyes went instantly to Nan. The pain that flashed in them didn't surprise me. Even though he acted like he didn't like her I knew he cared for Nan. She had been the needy little brat that was impossible not to love when we were growing up. Those kind of bonds are impossible to break.

"I just spoke with Woods. Blaire is okay. She was locked out of the house last night, but she stayed at Bethy's. I called Henrietta and she's unlocking the house for her." He spoke quietly as if he'd wake Nan or disturb her by talking about Blaire.

I'd left her standing in the driveway late at night alone. Thank God she had a phone. The idea of her being stranded in the dark was more than I could handle right now. "Is she upset?" With me, I wanted to add, but couldn't. How could she not be? I'd run out on her after screaming for her to get out of my car. When mom had told me about Nan something in me had switched and I'd lost it.

"Woods said he was going to look after her . . ." Grant trailed off. I knew what he was thinking. Leaving Woods to look after Blaire was dangerous. He was rich, successful and his family didn't hate her. What if she realized I was a waste of her time?

"She's pregnant," I told him. I had to tell someone.

"*Oh, hell*," he muttered and sank down onto the hard plastic chair that sat in the corner of the room. "When did you find out?"

"She told me shortly after she came back."

Grant covered his mouth and shook his head. That hadn't been something he expected to hear. But then he didn't know we were engaged either. He'd already left Rosemary when I'd proposed. I hadn't told him.

"That's why you proposed?" It wasn't really a question. It was more of a statement.

"You know about that?"

He shifted his eyes to Nan, "Yeah, Nan told me."

Nan had needed to vent I was sure. The fact she had chosen Grant to vent to was interesting. Normally those two were at each other's throats. Rarely did they spend quality time together.

"She wasn't happy about it," I said.

"No, she wasn't," he agreed.

I looked over at her and wished to God I could trade places with her right now. I hated that this was something I couldn't fix for her. I'd been fixing her problems her entire life. And now when she needed me most all I could do was sit here and stare at her helplessly.

"She thinks you've lost your mind. If she knew about the baby she'd think you asked Blaire just because of the baby."

"I didn't ask Blaire because of the baby. I asked her because I can't live without her. I just need Nan to understand that. I've spent my life making Nan happy. And now that I have found what makes me happy she can't accept it," I felt my throat close up and I shook my head. I was not going to cry.

Grant let out a deep sigh. "I think in time she will. Nan wants you to be happy too. She just thinks she knows what is best for you. Just like you think you know what is best for her." The tone in his voice as he said that last part was off. He'd meant something deeper than what he was saying. Or maybe I was just exhausted and needed to take a nap.

"I hope so," I replied then laid my head back on the chair and closed my eyes. "I need a nap. I can't keep this up. My head is getting fuzzy."

The chair he'd been sitting in scraped across the floor as he stood up. I listened as he walked across the room back toward the door. "Check in on Blaire for me. Please," I asked opening my eyes to make sure he was still there and heard me.

"I will," he assured me then walked out the door.

Two days later and still no sign of improvement. Nan wasn't waking up. I had gotten up to take a shower and change because my mother insisted. I couldn't deal with her and worry about Nan. I just did as she asked to shut her up.

Grant had sat in here with me most of the today. We hadn't talked much but having someone else here helped. My mother said she couldn't handle it and stayed at the hotel most of the time. Occasionally Abe would step in to check on her but I didn't expect any more from him. He never checked on the daughter he'd raised either. The man was missing a vital organ, a heart.

"I talked to Blaire," Grant said, breaking the silence. Just hearing her name made me ache. I missed her. I wanted her here but that would only upset everyone. I needed Nan better and when she woke up she didn't need to find Blaire here. It would only upset her.

"What did she sound like?" Did she hate me?

"Good. I guess. Maybe sad. She's worried about you and Nan. She asks about Nan before she asks about you. She also . . . she also asked if her father was okay today. Not sure why she cares but she did."

Because Blaire cared more than she should about everyone. Me included. She was too good for me and I was only going to keep hurting her. My family wouldn't accept her. The father that deserted her to marry my mom. Something I'd started with that damn picture. All I would ever do is hurt her in the long run.

"She has a doctor's appointment today. Woods told me he's taking her. She doesn't know I know about the baby."

Another appointment I was going to miss. How much longer was Blaire going to put up with this? I'd told her she and our baby came first, but this was the second time my family came before her doctor's appointment. And why the hell was Woods taking her?

"Why is Woods taking her? I have three vehicles in the garage."

Grant shot me an annoyed frown. "Yeah you do. But you never gave her permission to drive one and never told her where she could find the keys so she won't touch them. Woods has been her chauffer all damn week."

Fuck.

"I know you're hurting because of Nan. But if you don't snap out of this and contact Blaire I'm not sure she and your baby are going to be around when you decide to go home. Sure don't want my niece or nephew having the last name *Kerrington*," he snapped and stalked out of the room.

BLAIRE

I sat in the waiting room and tried hard not to look at the other pregnant women around me. There were three of us. The woman across from me was snuggled up against her husband's arm. He kept whispering into her ear making her smile. His hand never left her stomach. There was no possessiveness in his demeanor. Just protectiveness. It was if he was protecting his wife and child with that simple gesture.

The other lady was much further along than either of us and her baby was moving. Her husband had both his hands on her stomach as he stared at her in awe. There was a sweet worshipful look on his face. They were sharing a moment and just glancing over in that direction made me feel as if I were intruding on it.

Then there was me. With Woods. I had told him he didn't need to come with me but he said he'd like to. He wasn't going back in the exam room because I wasn't about to let him see me almost naked in a thin cotton exam robe, but he was going to sit in the waiting room.

He had fixed himself a cup of the complimentary coffee and since he'd only taken one sip I assumed it tasted horrible. I missed coffee. It would probably be delicious to me. I needed to buy some decaffeinated coffee.

"Blaire Wynn," the nurse called out from the doorway leading back to the exam rooms.

I stood up and smiled down at Woods, "I shouldn't be too long."

He shrugged, "I'm not in a hurry."

"Your husband can come back with you," the nurse said cheerily. My face was instantly warm. I knew without looking my cheeks were flushed.

"He's just a friend," I quickly corrected her.

This time she was the one turning pink. She obviously hadn't read over my record to see that I was single. "I'm so sorry. Uh, well he can come back too if he wants to hear the heart beat."

I shook my head. That was too personal. Woods was a friend but I wasn't ready to share something as important as my baby's heartbeat with him. Rush hadn't even heard the baby's heartbeat yet. "No, that's okay."

I didn't glance back at Woods because I was embarrassed for both of us. He was just helping out. Being labeled as the baby daddy hadn't been what he'd signed up for.

The exam didn't take long. This time I'd been able to hear the baby's heartbeat without them having to stick a wand inside me. It had been just as loud and sweet as before. The pregnancy was progressing well and I was cleared to go with an appointment for four weeks from now.

Walking back out into the waiting room I found Woods reading a Parenting magazine. He looked up at me and smiled sheepishly. "The reading material here is limited," he explained.

I stifled a laugh.

He stood up and we walked out of the door together.

Once we were in the car he looked over at me. "You hungry?"

I was actually, but the longer I spent with Woods the more uncomfortable I felt. I couldn't shake the feeling that Rush wouldn't like this. He had never liked me being around Woods much. Even though I had needed a ride I was starting to worry this was a bad idea. It was better if Woods just drove me back to Rush's house.

"I'm more tired than anything. Can you just take me back to Rush's?" I asked

"Of course," he replied with a smile. Woods was really easy to deal with. I liked that. I wasn't in the mood for difficult.

"Have you talked to Rush yet?" he asked.

That wasn't a question I wanted to answer. So much for not being difficult. I just shook my head. He didn't need an explanation and if he did too bad because I didn't have one. I'd broken down and called Rush two nights ago and it had gone directly to voice mail. I'd left him a message but he hadn't called back. I was beginning to wonder if he was hoping I'd just be gone when he returned. How long was I supposed to stay at his house?

"He isn't dealing with this well I imagine. He'll call you soon," Woods said. I could tell by the tone of his voice he didn't even believe what he was saying. It was just to make me feel better. I closed my eyes and pretended to sleep so he wouldn't say anymore. I didn't want to talk about this. I didn't want to talk about anything.

Woods turned the radio on and we drove in silence the rest of the way back to Rosemary. When the car came to a stop I opened my eyes to see Rush's house in front of me. I was back.

"Thank you," I said looking over at Woods. His expression was serious. I could tell he was thinking about something that he didn't want to share with me. I didn't need to ask to know what it was. He thought I should leave too. Rush wasn't going to call and there was a chance he may not come back. I couldn't just live in his house.

"Call me if you need anything," Woods said meeting my gaze.

I nodded but I'd already made up my mind I wasn't going to call him anymore. Even if Rush didn't care what I did it just didn't feel right. I opened the car door and stepped out. With a final wave I headed to the front door and back into the empty house.

RUSH

Seven days and Nan still hadn't opened her eyes. My mother was stopping by less and less. Grant was starting to be the only visitor that stayed around and showed up regularly. Abe stopped by once a day for only a few minutes at a time. It was Nan and me against the world once again.

"You need to call her," Grant said, breaking the silence. I knew who he was talking about. Blaire was constantly on my mind. I felt guilty as I sat here staring at my sister and all I could think about was Blaire.

"I can't," I replied, unable to look at him. He'd see that I'd given up hope if I did.

"This isn't fair to her. Woods said she isn't coming to the club anymore and she hasn't called him in three days. He keeps a check on things through Bethy but even Bethy isn't sure Blaire is going to stay much longer. You just need to call her."

Leaving me would be the best thing she ever did. How could I be what she deserved if I was torn between my sister and her all the time? I couldn't keep Nan safe. How could she trust me to keep her and our baby safe?

"She deserves better," I managed to say it aloud. Instead of just chanting it in my head.

"Yeah she probably does. But she wants you."

God that hurt. I wanted her too. I wanted our baby. I wanted that life I let myself pretend we could have. How could I give that to her if my sister never woke up? I'd be ridden with guilt and pain. I wouldn't be the man she deserved. This would eventually eat at me until I was worthless to anyone.

"I can't," was all I managed to say.

Grant swore and stood up slinging his jacket on the floor before he walked out of the room slamming the door behind him. He didn't understand. No one did. I just stared at the wall across from me. I was starting to go numb. I was losing everything I'd ever let myself love.

The door opened back up and I looked over expecting to see Grant. Instead it was Abe. I wasn't in the mood to see him. He'd deserted the two people I loved most in the world at some point in their lives.

"Why the fuck do you even come here? You don't give a shit," I snarled.

Abe didn't respond. He walked over to the chair that Grant had just vacated and sat down. He never sat down and stayed for any length of time. The fact he was going to right now didn't sit well with me. I needed to be alone.

"I do give a shit. Your mother doesn't know I'm here. She wouldn't approve of what I'm about to tell you. But I think you deserve to know."

There was nothing that man had to say that I wanted to hear but I remained silent and waited. The quicker he said what he wanted the sooner he'd be gone.

"Nanette isn't my daughter. Your mother has always known that. She wanted Nan to be mine but we both knew when she got pregnant that it was impossible. We'd been broken up for over eight months when she called me. She had just found out she was pregnant and she was scared. She was still in love with your dad which was why we broke up to begin with. I couldn't live up to the legend that was Dean Finlay. I wanted to be enough for someone. I never would be for Georgianna. But I loved her and she was worried about how she was going to manage another child. I was young and stupid so I went back to her and we talked about marriage. I told her I'd have to think about it." He stopped and looked over at me. I was still reeling from the fact that he wasn't Nan's father.

"Once I got there Georgie was leaving you with Dean whenever she could and still going out with friends as if she wasn't pregnant. She wouldn't tell me who the dad was. I had just about met my limit when Rebecca came to visit her." His eyes went soft and before he briefly closed. I'd never seen the man show that much emotion.

"She was gorgeous. Long blond hair that looked like it was spun by angels. The biggest green eyes I'd ever seen and so damn sweet. She loved you. She didn't like your mother taking you to Dean. She worried you weren't safe with a bunch of rock stars. She looked after you when your mother went out. She made you these pancakes with Mickey Mouse ears that you loved. I was drawn to her and I couldn't leave. Your mother used us both for a while. Rebecca wouldn't go because she worried about you. And I wouldn't . . . because I'd fallen in love with Becca." This was not the story my mother had told me. This wasn't the story I'd been led to believe all these years but now that I'd met Blaire . . . that I knew her . . . this made a hell of a lot more sense.

"Your mom came home one night drunk. She wasn't far along in her pregnancy and she announced that Dean was the daddy of this baby too. I was furious that she'd been drinking and even more furious that your father had done this yet again with no intention of doing right by Georgie. So I called him and told him I wanted to talk to him. The talk didn't go well. He said that the baby wasn't his. If it was his he'd gladly claim it, but it wasn't. Apparently your mother had been sleeping with the lead singer of Slacker Demon for over a month. The baby was Kiro's and well you've grown up around Kiro. You know him well enough to know he isn't father material."

Kiro was Nan's father? I buried my face in my hands as different memories came back to me. Kiro coming over late yelling and cursing at my mom about stealing his kid. Kiro calling my mom a cheap slut and hoping 'his girl' didn't end up the same way. I'd forgotten those things. Or I'd just blocked them out.

"Through this Becca and I got closer. Dean took you and swore he was going to take care of what was his. Your mother cursed and shoved Becca down a flight of stairs calling her names I will not repeat and told us both to leave after she caught me kissing Becca one night. We had to go after that. Becca cried a lot because she was worried about you. She always worried about you."

When he talked about Becca all I could see was Blaire's face. Her sweet innocent face and my chest felt like it was about to explode.

"I asked Becca to marry me. She agreed. Weeks after our honeymoon we found out she was pregnant with twins. Those girls were my world. I adored the ground they walked on just as much as I adored their mother. Never a day went by that I wasn't thankful for the life I'd been given." He stopped and choked on a sob.

"Then one day Val and I were driving back from shopping. We'd gone to get her some shoes for Volleyball. Her feet had grown over the summer, but Blaire's hadn't. They were identical but it was starting to look like Blaire may be the shorter one out of the two. We were laughing about me singing along to some silly boy band on the radio. I missed . . . I missed the red light. We were hit on Val's side of the car by a truck going eighty miles an hour." He stopped and ran a hand over his face to wipe the tears and let out another sob.

"I lost my baby girl. I hadn't been paying attention. But I also lost my wife who couldn't look at me and my other daughter who was only a shell of the girl she'd been. Then you showed up with that picture of Nanette and instead of sticking it out and being the man my girls needed me to be, I fled. I told myself they deserved more than I could give them. I'd never be able to forgive myself and move on and that seeing me everyday would only hurt them more. So, I left them. I hated myself. I still hate myself. But I'm a weak man. I should have stayed.

"When I found out Becca was sick I went on a drinking binge. The idea of a world without Becca in it was impossible for me to accept. But going to see my vibrant wife who I loved, and will always love, lying there dying wasn't something I could do. I'd buried my daughter. I couldn't bury my wife. So, because I was weak, I left my baby girl to bury her momma. I will never forgive myself for that either." He finally looked my way.

"All you see is a selfish man who only thinks of himself. You're right. I don't deserve anyone's love or forgiveness. I don't want it. Your mother and Nan wanted me. They both acted like they needed me. I could pretend with them. The truth is your mother is as lost and broken as I am. Maybe for different reasons, but we're both empty inside. I was going to come clean with all this and tell Nan three months ago. I couldn't continue this farce. I just wanted to go sit by my wife's grave and grieve. But then Blaire called me. She needed me, but I had nothing to give. So, I lied to her. I didn't know much about the man you'd become but I knew one thing. You loved fiercely. You would do anything for your sister. I had no doubt in my mind that the moment you laid eyes on Blaire that she'd get to you. The sweet gentle spirit that was in her mother is in Blaire. Val was me. But Blaire . . . she is my Becca. She is so much like her. No man can be around her and not love her. I wanted someone strong and capable of taking care of her. So I sent her to you." He wiped away the rest of his tears and he stood up. I was speechless.

"Don't become me. Don't let her down like I did. You only deserve what you make yourself worthy of. Do what I couldn't. Be a man." Abe turned and walked out without another word.

BLAIRE

I hadn't been asleep very long when the phone rang. It was the middle of the night and only a few people had my number. My stomach knotted up as I reached for my phone. It was Rush.

"Hello," I said almost afraid of what he'd called to tell me.

"Hey, it's me," his voice sounded like he'd been crying. Oh god . . . please don't let Nan be dead.

"Is she okay?" I asked hoping that this time God had actually heard my prayer.

"She's awake. She's a little disoriented, but she knew me when she opened her eyes so her memory is good."

"Oh, thank God," I sat down on the bed and decided I needed to try this praying thing a little more often.

"I'm sorry, Blaire. I'm so sorry," his voice was hoarse. I could hear the pain laced in his words and I didn't have to ask what he meant. This was it. He just couldn't say it.

"It's okay. Just take care of Nan. I'm really glad she's okay, Rush. You may not believe that but I've been praying. I wanted her to be okay," I needed him to believe me. Even if there was no love loss between Nan and I knew she was important to him.

"Thank you," he said. "I'm coming home. I'll be there no later than tomorrow night."

I wasn't sure if this meant he wanted me gone by then or would we do our goodbyes in person. Running would be so much easier. Not having to face him. It hurt bad enough on the phone. Seeing his face was going to be so hard but I couldn't let it destroy me. I had our baby to think about. This wasn't just about me anymore.

"I'll see you then," I replied.

"I love you." Hearing the words hurt more than anything else. I wanted to believe he did but it wasn't enough. The love he might feel for me wasn't enough.

"I love you too," I replied and hung up the phone before curling into a ball and crying myself to sleep.

The doorbell rang just as I was getting out of the shower. I grabbed the clothes I'd laid out to wear and quickly got dressed before wrapping my hair in a towel and hurrying downstairs.

When I opened the door and saw my father standing there I wasn't sure what to think. Had Rush sent him to get rid of me? No. Rush wouldn't do that. But why was he here?

"Hey, Blaire. I, uh, came to talk to you," he didn't look like he'd slept in days and his clothes were rumpled. Seeing the daughter he *did* love in the hospital dying must have been hard on him. I pushed that bitterness away. I wasn't going to think about that. He was Nan's dad too. At least he was there for her now even if he'd screwed her over the first part of her life.

"What about?" I asked not moving to let him in. I wasn't sure there was anything he had to say that I wanted to hear.

"It's about Nan . . . and you."

I shook my head, "Don't care. I'm not up for hearing anything you have to say. Your daughter woke up. I'm glad she didn't die," I started to close the door.

"Nan isn't my daughter," he said the only words that would stop me from slamming the door in his face. I let his words sink in as I slowly opened the door back up. What did he mean Nan wasn't his daughter?

I just stared at him. This made no sense.

"I need to tell you the truth. Rush is going to tell Nan when she's ready. But I wanted to be the one to tell you."

What did Rush know? Had he been lying to me? I wasn't sure I could breathe. "Rush?" I asked backing up in case I couldn't get a deep breath and ended up passing out. I needed to sit down.

"I told Rush everything yesterday. He had been told the same lie you had but he knows the truth now."

The truth. What was the truth? Was there a truth or was my entire existence a lie? I sank down onto the steps and stared up at the man I thought was my father as he stepped inside and closed the door behind him.

* * *

"I've always known Nan wasn't my daughter. More importantly your mother knew Nan wasn't my daughter. You're right, your mother would have never allowed me to leave my pregnant fiancé and run off with her. Not for anything. She almost didn't let me leave my ex-girlfriend who was pregnant with another man's child because she was worried about what would happen to Rush. Her heart was just as big as you know it was. Nothing you knew was a lie, Blaire. Nothing. The world you knew was not a lie."

"I don't understand. I know my momma wasn't involved in any of this. That was never a question in my mind. But I don't understand. If you aren't Nan's dad why did you leave us for them?"

"I met your mother while trying to help Georgianna deal with her latest problem. Your mother had come to help her friend too. We both cared about her, she'd needed us and we tried to help. But while she was out partying and acting like she didn't have a little boy at home to take care of or that she was pregnant again, I fell in love with your mother. She was everything Georgianna wasn't. I adored her and for whatever reason she fell in love with me. When we left, Dean had come to take Rush and Kiro, the lead singer of Slacker Demon and Nan's real father had stepped in to offer his assistance. Georgianna found out about Becca and I. She sent us packing and we gladly went. Your mother worried over Rush and called Dean to check on him for awhile."

"Mom knew Rush?" Picturing my mother taking care of

Rush as a little boy stuck with two screwed up parents brought tears to my eyes. He'd known how wonderful my mother was once even if he didn't remember.

"Yeah. He called her Beck Beck. He preferred her over Georgianna and that didn't settle well with Georgie either. Once she got Rush back she refused to let your mother check on him. Your mother cried for weeks worrying over the little boy she'd grown to love. But that was your mom. Always caring too much. Her heart was bigger than anyone I'd ever known . . . until you. You're just like her sweetheart."

I held up my hands to stop him. We would not be bonding over this. I wasn't crying because I knew my mother was innocent of the lies she'd been falsely accused of. I was crying because she'd loved Rush once too. That his entire childhood hadn't been lonely.

"I'm almost done. Let me finish then I'll leave and you'll never see me again. I swear."

He knew I was leaving too. That this thing with Rush and me was over. The sharp pain in my chest was almost too much.

"Val's death was my fault. I ran that red light. I hadn't been paying attention and I lost one of my girls that day. But I lost you and your mother too. You were both hurting so bad and it was all my fault. I wasn't man enough to stay and bear seeing you both in so much pain. So I ran. I let you take care of Becca when it should have been me but I was too weak. I couldn't stand the thought of seeing my Becca sick. It would end me. I drank myself into a stupor. It was the only way to stay numb.

Then you called and said she'd died. My Becca wasn't on this earth any longer. I was going to tell Nan the truth about her father and I was going to leave. I wasn't sure where I'd go but I didn't care if I lived or died.

"Then you called and needed me. I wasn't even a man anymore. I was worthless. But I couldn't let you down. I'd already made you suffer so much alone. I sent you to Rush. He wasn't exactly the kind of guy a man wants his daughter around, but I knew he'd see in you what I saw in Becca. A lifeline. A reason to live. A reason to fight. A reason to change. He was strong. He could protect you and I knew if pushed he would."

This was all too much. I couldn't make sense of it. He had sent me to Rush? The guy who adored a sister who hated me and blamed me for everything wrong in her life?

"He hated me," I told him. "He hated who I was."

My father's smile was sad. "Yes he hated who you were, but then he met you. He was around you and that was all it took. You are rare, Blaire. Just as your mother was. There aren't many people in this world as strong as you are. As full of love and willing to forgive. You always envied the way Val could charm a room. You thought she got the best out of the two of you. But what Val and I knew was that we were the lucky ones because we had people like you and your mother in our lives. Val adored you. She saw that you were the one that had your mother's spirit. We stood in awe of the both of you. I still do and although all I've done is hurt you since the day we lost your sister, I have loved you. I always will. You're my little girl. You deserve the best in this world and I'm not the best. I'm walking away and I'm not going to ever bother you again. I need to live out the rest of this life alone. Remembering what I once had."

The grief in his eyes tore at my soul. He was right. He'd deserted me and momma when we needed him the most. But maybe we'd deserted him too. We hadn't gone after him. We'd just let him go. The day we lost Valerie had marked all our lives. Momma and Val were gone now and we could never get them back. But we were here. I didn't want to live the rest of my life knowing my father was out there somewhere alone. My momma wouldn't want that. She never wanted him to be alone. She loved him until she drew her last breath. Val wouldn't want that. She'd been a daddy's girl.

I stood up and took a step toward him. The unshed tears in his eyes slowly began to trickle down his face. He was a shell of the man he once was but he was my dad. A sob tore from my chest and I threw myself into his arms. When they wrapped around me and held me tightly I let all the pain free. I cried for the life we lost. I cried for him because he wasn't strong enough and I cried for me because it was time.

RUSH

The house was dark and silent when I unlocked the door and stepped inside. Would Blaire have turned out all the lights if she were here alone? I'd been so focused on getting home to her after talking with Nan that I hadn't let myself consider she could have left me. Would she have left me?

I turned and took the stairs two at a time. Once I hit the top step I started running. My heart was pounding in my chest. She couldn't be gone. I'd told her I loved her. I'd told her I was coming home. She had to be here. I had to tell her everything. I had to tell her things would be different. I had to tell her I remembered her mom. I remembered those Mickey Mouse pancakes. I had to tell her I was going to be the man she needed. I was going to be the best damn father the world had ever known.

I jerked the door open leading up to my room and darted up the steps needing to see her. God let her be there. Please let her be there.

The bed was empty. No! I scanned the room for her things. Something to tell me she hadn't left me. She couldn't have left me. I'd chase her down. I'd get on my knees and grovel. I'd be her damn shadow until she gave in and forgave me.

"Rush?" her voice broke the silence and the pounding in my head and I spun around to see her sitting up on the sofa. Her hair was a tangled mess and her sleepy face was perfect.

"You're here," I went to her and fell down on my knees and dropped my head in her lap. She was here. She hadn't left me.

Her hands touched my head as she ran her hands through my hair. "Yes, I'm here," she replied in an unsure voice.

I was scaring her, but I just needed a minute to reassure myself she hadn't left me. I hadn't completely messed this up. I didn't want to be like her dad. The lost and empty man I'd seen yesterday wasn't someone I ever wanted to become. And I knew without Blaire I'd be just like that.

"Are you okay?" she asked.

I nodded but kept my head in her lap. She continued to try and soothe me by gently stroking my head. When I was sure I could talk to her without completely breaking down I lifted my head to look up at her.

"I love you," the way I said it was so fierce it almost sounded like I was swearing.

A small sad smile tugged at her lips. "I know and it's okay. I understand. I'm not going to make you choose. I just want you to be happy. You deserve to be happy. I've had a lot of time to think about it and I'm going to be fine. You don't have to worry about me. I'm strong. I can do this on my own."

I wasn't following what she was saying. What was she doing on her own? "What?" I asked replaying her words back in my head.

"I talked to my dad today. I know everything. It's hard to comprehend but it all makes more sense now."

Abe had come here? He'd come and told her everything. She knew . . . but what she was saying still made no sense.

"Baby, maybe it's because I haven't slept much in the past eight days or because I'm so fucking relieved that you're here, but I don't understand what you're trying to tell me."

A tear glistened in her eye and I jumped up and pulled her into my lap. I didn't want to make her cry. I thought this was a happy thing. She knew the truth that she'd always known, her mom was as pure and honest as she believed. I was home and I was ready to be everything she deserved in life. I'd die making her happy.

"I love you and because I love you I am letting you go. I want you to get out of life what you want. I don't want to be a chain around your leg."

"What did you just say?" I asked as the words 'letting go' sank in. Like hell she was letting me go.

"You heard me, Rush. Don't make this harder than it is," she whispered.

I stared at her in disbelief. She really meant what she was saying. I'd left her here to think all kinds of things while I'd set in the hospital with Nan. I should have called but I hadn't. Of course she was confused.

"Listen to me, Blaire. If you try to go anywhere I will chase you down. I will become your shadow. I won't let you out of my sight because I can't live without you. I made so many damn mistakes with you I don't even want to try and count them but I am going to start making things right from here on out. I swear to you that this won't happen again. I know now that this is where I'm supposed to be. No more lies. Just us."

She sniffled and buried her head in my shoulder. I pulled her tighter up against me. "I mean it. I need you. You can't leave me."

"But I don't fit. Your family hates me. I make your life difficult."

That's where she was wrong. "No. *You're* my family. My mother has never been my family. She has never even tried to be. My sister may not have completely come around, but she did tell me to ask you if she was going to be able to be apart of her niece or nephew's life. So she's getting there. And as for making my life difficult. You, Blaire Wynn, make my life complete."

Blaire's mouth covered mine as she grabbed fistfuls of my shirt. Her tongue slid into my mouth and I savored the taste of her. I'd missed her so much. How I could have thought for a minute I'd survive without this . . . without her, I don't know.

BLAIRE

"I need to be inside you," Rush whispered in my ear as he kissed along my jawline and slid his hands up under my tank top.

"Good," I replied reaching for his shirt and pulling it over his head. He chuckled and lifted his hands to make it easier then pulled my top off too.

"Damn, they've grown since I've been gone," he murmured cupping each of my breasts in his hands. "Is there . . . like milk in them already?" he asked.

"No," I giggled.

"I'm trying real hard not to be a man about this but I can't help it. I'm real fucking excited about these," he admitted before looking up at me through his eyelashes as he pulled a nipple into his mouth.

"Oh," I moaned and grabbed his head to hold him there. Somehow they'd grown even more sensitive. With each tug of his mouth my clit throbbed. It was like there was a direct line between the two.

"Get these panties off," Rush said with his mouth full as he tugged at my panties. I eased up and slid them down with his help. He only let go of one nipple to suck on the other.

"Fuck," he groaned sliding a finger inside me. "It's wet. Always so wet and ready."

I reached for his buckle and started unfastening his jeans. I wanted him naked too.

"Not yet," he said moving me off his lap to lay me back on the sofa. " I need a taste."

I watched as he pushed my legs apart and lowered his head to lick right through the center of my folds.

"Oh, God! Rush!" I cried out lifting my hips to get closer to his mouth. The barbell slid over my clit as he flicked it against my swollen bud over and over. Driving me crazy.

"I love it when you squirm," he said with a wicked grin. I loved it when he made me squirm.

His finger slid into my heat as he continued to torture my clit with his tongue piercing. This wild sexy man was mine. It was hard to comprehend at times but I was so glad I showed up at his door four months ago.

He stood up and pushed his jeans and boxer briefs down stepping out of them. I stared up at him. He was beautiful. I let my eyes roam over his body. Nothing could make him any more perfect. Except . . . "Rush?"

"Yeah."

"Could you get your nipples pierced?" I asked surprising myself at the request.

Rush laughed as he came back over me. "You want my nipples pierced now do you?"

I nodded and slid my hands up his chest and ran my thumbs over his nipples. "I like your other piercings."

He kissed my neck and ran his hand down my leg until he hooked his arm under my knee and pulled my leg up. "Will you kiss it and make it better? 'Cause I'm thinking that's gonna hurt like a motherfucker."

"I promise to make it feel very good," I smiled up at him.

"Anything you want, baby. Just don't ask me to pierce anything south of my waist.

I raised my eyebrows. I hadn't thought of that. Before I could say anything else Rush was pushing inside me and all other thoughts left me. He was filling me and stretching me and everything was perfect in the world again.

"Fuck! How did you get tighter?" Rush panted over me as his arms trembled from holding back.

I threw my head back and lifted my hips. It was better. I didn't think this could get better. "It's more sensitive," I managed to say on a strangled cry.

"Does it hurt?" he asked pulling back. I grabbed his ass and held him in me.

"NO! It's good. It's really good. Harder, Rush. Please. It feels incredible."

Rush groaned and plunged the rest of the way inside me.

"I'm not gonna last long. It's too tight. I'm gonna come." He stopped moving and slowly eased back. I was so close. I didn't want him to slow down. The sensation each thrust sent through me was amazing. I needed more of it. I pushed him back and with all the strength I had. He sat back watching me while I quickly climbed on him and sank down on him hard and fast.

"Holy SHIT!" He yelled grabbing fistfuls of my hair.

I pumped up and down on him as my body climbed closer to that ecstasy it was promising me was close.

"Baby, I'm gonna come, ARRRRGGGGHHHH!" Rush called out then grabbed my face and kissed me with a fierceness that sent me over the edge with him. Crying out in his mouth I shook with release as he held me tightly tasting me and sucking my tongue into his mouth.

I collapsed on him and he held me close to him. We sat there breathing hard in silence. My vagina kept contracting as if my body was experiencing aftershocks. Each time it did Rush groaned.

When I was sure I could talk again I tilted my head back and looked up at him. "What just happened?" I asked him.

He laughed and shook his head. "I don't know. You just fucked the hell out of me. I swear that one is going down in the books baby. I didn't think it could get any better and you just proved me wrong. Holy hell you were wild."

I buried my face in his chest and laughed with him. I had been a little out of control.

"This better not be a pregnant thing or your hot little ass is gonna live knocked up for the next thirty years."

RUSH

I held Blaire's hand in mine and looked over her shoulder as she flipped through a parenting magazine. All the pictures of diapers and other baby items were scary as shit. I wouldn't admit that to her but the reality of a baby was starting to terrify me. The big boobs, the middle of the night sex and the sweet swell of Blaire's hips were all major pluses and it was easy to forget exactly why all this was happening.

"Blaire Wynn," the nurse called out her name and I looked down at the diamond on her finger. In two weeks that last name would change. I was ready for it. I didn't like her being called Wynn. She was Blaire Finlay to me already.

"That's us," she said smiling up at me before standing. She was barely showing now. How they expected to see more than an even bigger pea I wasn't sure but she was promising me we could actually see the baby. It had arms and legs as crazy as that sounded.

I didn't let go of her hand as she led us back to the exam room. The nurse glanced back at me several times. She had better not be about to tell me I couldn't go back there because I was going. It was time I saw my baby.

"In here," the nurse said stepping back and waving us into a room. "Go ahead and take everything off and put on the gown. Doctor Nelson will want to do a vaginal exam today too. But we'll get to the ultrasound first."

Blaire seemed to not think it was a big deal she was about to have to get naked. The nurse looked back at me. "Is this one okay to be back here?"

This one? What the hell did that mean?

Blaire grinned and looked back at me. "Yes this one is the father.

The nurse straightened up and gave me a big relieved smile. "That's wonderful. I hated the idea of someone as young as you doing this all alone."

Blaire blushed and went into a small room with a curtain in front of it. Once the nurse left I went over and stepped into what looked like a small dressing room.

"What did she mean by 'this one'?" I asked.

Blaire bit her bottom lip and closed her eyes tightly. "Do I have to answer this?"

"Uh, yeah especially after that comment," I was preparing myself not to like the answer.

"Woods drove me to my last appointment. They told him he could come back and I told them no he couldn't he was just a friend."

I'd almost forgotten about that. I understood why she had gotten a ride from him. I hadn't been here. But knowing some other man was here with her when she needed me was hard to swallow. I realized her face had gone pale and I bent down and kissed her lips. "It's okay. I should've been here. I wasn't."

She nodded. "I'm sorry."

"Don't be. I'm the one who's sorry."

The door to the exam room opened back up and I stuck my head out of the dressing room.

The nurse was grinning at me and pulling in a machine with a little screen on it. "Is she about ready?" the amused smirk on the nurse's face was funny.

"Just about," I told her then looked back at Blaire who was bright red. I couldn't help but laugh. "Get changed sexy. I'll go back out there."

Blaire nodded and I stepped out from behind the curtain.

I walked over to the table and looked at the machine. "So this is how we see the baby?" I asked wondering how they did this exactly.

"Yep. Because Blaire's on Medicaid we have to use this one. This is all Medicaid will cover. We have a newer 4D one that I wish Medicaid would cover because you can see the baby so clearly. But it doesn't."

I paused and looked from the machine to the nurse. Blaire was on Medicaid? What the hell? I hadn't even thought about the fact she needed insurance. I'd always had the best money could buy it wasn't something I thought about.

"I want the 4D machine. I'll pay whatever it cost right now but I want the very best this office can supply."

The nurse glanced from my earrings to Tshirt that had seen it's better days. It was one my dad had given me after one of his tours about five years ago. I liked it because it was a tight fit and Blaire seemed to like tight shirts on me.

"I . . . uh . . . I don't think you understand exactly how much an ultrasound like that cost. While it is very sweet that you want to give that experience to Blaire it is very—"

"I can afford any procedure available. I told you I'd pay for it now. I want the best ultrasound for Blaire and my baby."

The nurse started to open her mouth when Blaire walked out of the room wearing a thin cotton robe. "Please don't argue with him. He'll cause you problems if you do. Just get me the 4D ultrasound."

The nurse shrugged, "Okay if you're sure but he'll need to prepay."

I opened my wallet and handed her my American Express black card. Her eyes shot up and she nodded then hurried from the room.

"I should tell you now that I was perfectly okay with a regular ultrasound, but that would be a lie. I've seen pictures of 4D ultrasounds in those Parenting magazines and I really want one."

Blaire was grinning like a kid who was about to go to Disney World for the first time. Hell to get her to smile like that I'd go buy the fucking 4D machine.

"My girl and my kid get the best. Always."

The door opened back up and the nurse walked in staring at me now like she was trying to figure something out. She handed me my card. I took it and slipped it back in my wallet.

"Are you Dean Finlay's son?" the woman finally asked.

"Yeah. Now let's go see my baby," I replied.

The women nodded eagerly and turned to look at Blaire. "The 4D machine is in a special room. Are you comfortable walking through the hall in that robe?"

"Will someone see her?" I asked stepping in front of her because I sure as hell wasn't comfortable with it.

The nurse opened a cabinet and pulled out a blanket. "Here wrap this around her."

I wrapped Blaire up in it until she was completely covered. She was pressing her lips together trying not to laugh. I winked at her and pressed a kiss to her nose.

We walked down a long hallway where we passed two nurses, another couple and Blaire's doctor who asked why we were moving. The nurse quickly told him that I'd just paid for the 4D and the doctor looked very pleased as he followed us into the room.

Blaire lay down on a table and they began prepping her as I sat patiently waiting. Once they had her stomach bare the nurse put some clear gel on her stomach then looked back at me. "Are you two wanting to know the sex of the baby?"

"Ask the momma," I replied.

"I'd like to know," Blaire said glancing back at me for reassurance.

“Me too,” I agreed.

Then the doctor began moving something over Blaire’s stomach and a small beating noise filled the air. “Is that my baby’s heartbeat,” I asked, standing up because sitting was no longer possible. My heart was beating as fast as the one I heard on the screen.

“Yes it is,” the doctor replied. “And there . . . and there he is,” he said.

I stared at the screen as a small little life began to take shape.

“He?” Blaire asked.

“Yes, it’s most definitely a boy,” the doctor replied.

I reached out and grabbed Blaire’s hand unable to take my eyes off the screen. That was our baby. I was gonna have a son. Fuck . . . I was also gonna cry.

Want To Know What Happens Next?

Turn The Page For An Exclusive Preview Of The Third Instalment In Rush And Blaire's Hot Romance . . .

Forever Too Far.

PROLOGUE

If I hadn't been so taken in by Blaire and the way she lit up the place, I would have seen him walk in. But I hadn't. It wasn't until the talking surrounding me went silent and eyes all stared at the door my back was to. Glancing down at Blaire who was still talking to Woods and didn't notice the change in the room, I moved her behind me in a protective measure before turning around to see what had captured the bars attention.

The same silver eyes that I saw every day in the mirror were focused on me. It had been awhile since I'd seen my dad. Normally we kept in contact more but with Blaire coming into my world and completely turning it on its axis, I hadn't taken the time and energy to track my father down so I could talk to him.

It looked like he had come to find me this time.

"That's your father," Blaire said quietly beside me. She'd moved from where I'd tucked her behind me and was holding onto my arm now.

"Yeah, it is."

BLAIRE

Without stage makeup and black leather clothing he looked like an older version of Rush. I had to move quickly to keep up with Rush who had my hand clasped tightly in his as he walked swiftly outside away from the other guests in the bar. His father led the way. I wasn't sure if Rush was happy to see him or not. The only interaction they'd had was Rush nodding his head towards the door. He obviously hadn't wanted this introduction to have an audience.

Dean Finlay, the world's most notorious drummer, stopped several times on our way out to autograph items being shoved in front of him. It wasn't just females either. One guy had even stepped forward and asked him to sign a bar napkin. The threatening gleam in Rush's eyes as he tried to get his father out of the bar kept the rest of them away. Instead, they all remained silent and watched as Slacker Demon's drummer headed out the door.

The night breeze was cold now. I immediately shivered and Rush stopped and wrapped his arms around me. "We need to go to the house. I'm not going to make her stand out here and talk. It's too damn cold." Rush told his father.

Dean finally stopped walking and looked back at me. His eyes slowly took me in and I could see the moment he noticed my stomach.

"Dean, this is Blaire Wynn. My fiancée. Blaire, this is Dean Finlay, my father." Rush said in a tight voice. He didn't sound like he wanted to make this introduction.

"No one told me I was gonna be a grandpa," Dean said in a slow drawl. I wasn't sure how he felt about that because there was no emotion on his face.

"I've been busy," was the only response Rush gave him. That was odd. Was he embarrassed to tell his dad? I felt sick in my stomach and started to ease away from him.

His arms tightened their hold on me and I could feel his attention focused completely on me. "What's wrong?" Rush asked, turning his back on his father and bending down so he could look me directly in the eyes.

I didn't want to have this conversation in front of Dean. I could feel his dad's eyes on both of us. I shook my head but my body was still tense. I couldn't help that. The fact he hadn't told his father was bothering me.

"I'm taking her to the car. I'll meet you back at the house," Rush said over his shoulder but kept his eyes focused on mine. I dropped my gaze wishing I hadn't reacted now. I was making a scene. Dean was going to think I was a whinny princess.

I opened my mouth to argue when Rush wrapped his arm around my waist and led me to the Range Rover. He was anxious. He didn't like me upset, which was something we needed to work on. I would get upset. He couldn't control that.

Rush opened the passenger side door and lifted me up and put me in like I was five. When he thought I was upset he started treating me like a child. We really needed to work on that too.

He didn't even have his door closed before he looked at me. "Something is wrong. I need to know so I can fix it."

I sighed and sank back against the seat. I might as well get this over with even if I was being a little touchy. "Why haven't you told your dad about the baby?"

Rush reached over and closed his hand over mine. "That's what's wrong? You're upset because I haven't told Dean?"

I nodded and kept my eyes on our hands resting on my leg.

"I haven't taken time to track him down. And I knew he'd show up when I told him because he'd want to meet you. I wasn't ready for company just yet. Especially him."

I was being silly. Lately my emotions were on high alert. I lifted my eyes and met his concerned gaze. "Okay. I understand that."

Rush leaned over and kissed my lips gently. "I'm sorry I upset you," he whispered before pressing one more kiss to the corner of my lips and leaning back. It was moments like these that I became a swoony mess.

"He's here now. So, let's go see what brought him here before my mother finds out. I want you to myself. I don't like having my fucked up family around."

Rush didn't let go of my hand as he cranked the engine and pulled out onto the road. I laid my head against the seat and turned it so I could look at him. His unshaven jaw made him look older and untamed. Very sexy. I wish he'd not shave more often. I liked the way it felt too. He had taken out his earring and hardly ever wore it anymore.

"Why do you think he's here?" I asked

Rush glanced over at me. "I was hoping he was here to meet you. But I don't think he knew about you yet. He looked surprised. So that means this could very well be about Nan."

Nan. His sister hadn't been back to Rosemary since she was released from the hospital. Rush didn't seem to be worried about it but he loved his sister. I hated being the reason she stayed away. Now that she knew who her real father was and that I had never taken anything away from her, I'd hoped we could be friends for Rush's sake. It wasn't looking like that was going to happen.

"Do you think Nan has gone to see Kiro?" I asked.

Rush shrugged. "I don't know. She seems different since her accident."

The car came to a stop outside the large beach house that had been purchased for Rush by his father when he was just a kid.

Rush squeezed my hand. "I love you, Blaire. I'm so damn proud of the fact you're going to be the mother of my son. I want everyone to know. Never doubt that."

My eyes stung with tears and I nodded before picking up his hand kissing it. "I get emotional. You need to ignore me when I get like that."

Rush shook his head. "I can't ignore you. I want to reassure you."

The passenger side door opened and I jerked my head around to see Dean Finlay standing there with a smirk on his face. "Let the woman out of the car, son. It's time I met the mother of my grandchild."

Dean held out his hand and I put mine in his not sure what else to do. His long fingers wrapped around my hand and he helped me down out of the Range Rover. Rush was there immediately, taking my hand from his father's and pulling me over to him. His dad chuckled and shook his head. "I'll be damned."

"Let's get inside." Rush replied.